They Said
He Killed A Hero

*When Wes Tancred shot Sam Older, the legend-
ary hero who supposedly robbed the rich and gave
to the poor, he was labeled a sneaking killer despite his claim he had done it in self-defense. And
so he rode the West alone, hiding from his shame.*

And then the day came when Sage City was ripped
wide open by Hong Kong Smith and his crew of
Texas outlaws. The town's marshal turned in his
badge when the shooting started, and bet his life
on the wrong man. Other town big shots sided
with the lawless desperadoes who might make
them rich. But Laura Vesser loved Wes Tancred
despite his protests he could no longer return love.

**And so Wes strapped on his guns again. Lots of
things were to change before the Sage City showdown came to a blazing finish!**

⊘ A Signet Brand Western

SIGNET Brand Westerns You'll Enjoy

Bitter Sage

by

Frank Gruber

A SIGNET BOOK

NEW AMERICAN LIBRARY

TIMES MIRROR

SIGNET TRADEMARK REG. U.S. PAT. OFF. AND FOREIGN COUNTRIES
REGISTERED TRADEMARK—MARCA REGISTRADA
HECHO EN CHICAGO, U.S.A.

SIGNET, SIGNET CLASSICS, MENTOR, PLUME AND MERIDIAN BOOKS
are published by The New American Library, Inc.,
1633 Broadway, New York, New York 10019

FIRST PRINTING, OCTOBER, 1973

3   4   5   6   7   8   9   10   11

PRINTED IN THE UNITED STATES OF AMERICA

Chapter 1

During The War Between The States, Sam Older rode with the infamous Quantrell. He raided and looted and killed and he was with his chief at the bloody massacre of Lawrence. After the war when even the guerrillas received amnesty and returned to peaceful pursuits, Sam Older became an outlaw. He held up banks and robbed trains.

Then Sam Older was killed and became The Great American Legend, the man who was hounded into outlawry and stole from the rich to give to the poor.

The name of Wes Tancred, the man who killed Sam Older, became an epithet.

The sheriff unlocked the cell door and pulled it open. He said, "All right, Tancred."

Wes Tancred got up from the cot and looked uncertainly at the sheriff. It was scarcely two hours since the judge had delivered the sentence. It couldn't be so soon. It was always a matter of days, weeks.

The sheriff held out a folded paper. "Here it is."

Tancred took the sheet, unfolded it. He saw the seal in the upper right corner, the words, *Office Of The Governor,* but the body of the letter suddenly became a blur. There was no need to read, however. The sheriff told him the contents of the governor's letter.

A full pardon.

"You were expecting it, weren't you?" the sheriff asked. "It was part of the deal. . . ."

"Deal?"

"Ten thousand dollars reward—and amnesty." The sheriff held up a hand to stop Tancred's denial. "I know. You said it at the trial. There was no deal." He turned away. "Come on."

Tancred followed the sheriff into his office. There the lawman opened a wooden box and took out the contents. Twelve dollars and fifty-five cents, a clasp knife and a Navy Colt.

"Your property."

Tancred picked up the money. He looked at the knife, hesitated, then put it into his hip pocket. The sheriff shoved the revolver across the desk with the heel of his hand.

"Someday you'll be able to sell that for a good price. The gun that killed Sam Older."

"Can I go now?" Tancred asked.

"Why not? You're as free as the birds."

Tancred stuck the Navy Colt under the waistband of his trousers and started for the door. As he touched the knob, the sheriff said, "There are a bunch of reporters outside. You can sneak out the back way."

Tancred turned, crossed the room and went through a door. He missed the reporters who were waiting out front . . . and faced Helen Older.

She was only twenty-four but she looked thirty. She said to him, "Remember it, Wes Tancred. Think of it every day of your life. How you murdered him in cold blood, for ten thousand silver dollars."

He cried out hoarsely, "No, Helen, it wasn't like that. You must believe me. It wasn't like they said. I didn't plan it. I didn't make a deal. I—I'm not taking a cent of the money."

"Take it, Wes, you earned it. Take it and may the food you buy with it taste like ashes, the whiskey like vinegar. May everything you touch turn to blood. And think of Sam, think of him every day of your life. Listen—listen to his voice in the night. See him wherever you go and hear him, hear him always, cursing you for a blackhearted traitor . . . and *murderer!*"

She turned then and walked away.

Chapter 2

Life has to be lived.

Tancred rode the lonely trails. He saw Dakota and Wyoming, he rode through Kansas and Colorado. He went to Texas and Louisiana, Illinois and Kentucky, Ohio and Missouri. He visited towns and cities, he rode for days without seeing another human being. Countless nights he spread his blankets under the stars and stared at the heavens above. A thousand hours he tossed in a bed and could not sleep.

He had to live, so he worked. He worked as a laborer on the railroad as it crept across Nebraska and Wyoming. He went deep into the bowels of the earth in the silver mines of Colorado. He sold shoes in a store and once he read law in an attorney's office, but mostly he worked as a printer, a trade at which he had had some apprenticeship back in Missouri before . . . before he had killed Sam Older.

He lived.

Nine years dragged by and in the spring of 1876 a doctor in Michigan listened to his heart and tapped his chest and his lungs and said, "Get rid of the tension, get out in the sun and work with your hands. Forget everything that's ever worried you and relax. If not. . . ."

The doctor knew him as John Bailey. A lot of people had known him by that name and quite a few of them had talked to Bailey . . . about the blackhearted traitor who had killed the great Sam Older, the sneaking youth who had caught the most desperate man of his time by surprise and put a bullet through his head. Someone wrote a song about it and the man who called himself John Bailey heard it. It was an extremely popular ballad and men sang it everywhere. Men and women sang it. Bailey heard it a thousand times.

And the doctor told him to get rid of the tension! He did not know that John Bailey was Wes Tancred.

Well, one place was as good as another. And one job paid almost as much as another, so now in the spring of 1877, the man who called himself John Bailey looked over the log poles of the corral behind the stage station and saw a hundred miles of Kansas prairieland.

He watered the horses and he fed them. He rubbed them down and he hitched them to the once-a-week stage as it paused for moments every Thursday on its way to Kansas & Western a hundred miles to the south. He drove the relieved horses into the corral and rubbed them down and fed and watered them and tended them, and on Saturday he hitched them to the north-bound stage as it stopped for moments on its run to the Union Pacific two hundred and twenty miles to the north.

The job was an easy one and it kept him in the open. He slept in the shed by the corral when it rained and when the stars shone he moved out under them. And when there was no work to be done, which was most of the time, he sat in the sun and watched the sod-covered stage station.

And Laura Vesser.

Laura was twenty, a slim, fresh girl with the bluest of blue eyes and a freckled nose. She had lived here with her father at this lonely spot on the Kansas plains for six years. It was a sorry life for a girl, but Vesser had no relatives in the east with whom she could live and he had only one lung and could not live in the towns. So he kept this miserable sod-house and horse relay station for the stage line and wondered what Laura would do when his second lung was gone.

Perhaps. . . .

When John Bailey came along and indicated a willingness to stay and help with the horses, Vesser offered him pay from his own paltry wage and when Laura's eyes brightened every time she saw the hostler, Vesser felt more at peace with himself.

Yet . . . what was it about Bailey?

He wasn't old, but his eyes were weary and always there was a faraway look in them. He did his work and he was there and always his eyes watched Laura, but in six weeks he had spoken no words to her that he could not have said to her before strangers. And Laura's smile was sometimes strained.

Then one Wednesday morning the three men came out of the north and tied their horses to the corral poles.

They were whiskered and unkempt and none had washed for days. They were ravenously hungry and they ate every scrap of the food Laura cooked and set before them and no word was said about payment for the food. They asked for whiskey.

"I don't sell it here," Vesser told them.

"Who said anything about selling?" sneered the worst looking one of the trio, a man the others called Jethro. "We ain't got two dollars between us."

"We still want the whiskey," said the smallest of the three, a squat, ugly man with snaggled teeth.

Vesser shook his head. "I've no whiskey to give you."

Dave, the third man, who might have been the leader of the trio, a cold-eyed man in his early thirties, got up from the table and went into the lean-to where Laura did the cooking.

Angrily, Vesser started after him. The squat man sprang up from the table and cut off Vesser.

"Don't," he said.

Vesser swerved to the wall where a Sharp's rifle was suspended across two wooden pegs. Jethro came up as Vesser reached for the gun. He clouted him a hard blow with his fist.

Laura screamed and the squat man lunged for her, but Laura evaded his grab and made the open door.

Outside, Tancred was coming toward the station from the corrals.

"John!" Laura cried. "Those men. . . ."

The squat man came out of the stage station, a Navy revolver in his grimy fist.

"Don't make no play, bub," he said.

Tancred held up his hands, palms forward.

"I've no gun."

The squat man showed his bad teeth in a wicked grin. "Good thing you ain't got one."

Vesser came hurtling out of the stage station, propelled by Jethro who followed with Vesser's Sharp's rifle. He looked coolly at Tancred, then with a sudden hard blow, smashed the gun barrel over a rock, cracking it. He threw it to the ground.

"Just so we don't have no trouble."

The leader of the trio came out with a flask of whiskey. "Your cooking whiskey, I suppose," he remarked.

Vesser said, bitterly, "All right, you've had food and you've got the whiskey. Pile on your horses. . . ."

"Uh-uh," said Jethro. "Not just yet."

"There's nothing here to hold you."

The man with the whiskey regarded Vesser coldly. "The south stage stops here tomorrow, doesn't it?"

Vesser understood the question and made no reply.

The squat man said, "Dave asked you a question."

"I heard it," replied Vesser testily.

"Then answer him."

Tancred saw that Vesser would not answer and as the squat man moved in on him, Tancred said, "Yes, the stage comes through here on Thursday, usually around two o'clock in the afternoon."

Dave grinned wolfishly. "You've got more sense than he has." He inclined his head at his companions and headed for the corral. They followed. When they were out of earshot, Vesser said to Tancred, "You shouldn't have told them."

"What difference does it make? They can see it coming ten miles away."

"I know, but . . ."

"They'd have killed you, Dad," said Laura.

Vesser exhaled heavily. "They're going to hold up the stage."

Tancred nodded agreement.

Vesser's forehead creased. "The rifle's out of commission," He paused a moment. "I've got a revolver—if they don't search my bed."

"No!" Tancred said, quickly. "You can't fight them. Fighting is their business."

"John's right, Dad," said Laura, worriedly. "The company doesn't expect you to fight bandits."

"I can't just stand by and watch them hold up the stage."

From the corral, Dave called, "You . . . the hostler! Come here. . . ."

"Be careful," Tancred said to Vesser and turning, walked over to the corral.

The three men had opened the bottle and passed it around once. Jethro was taking his second drink as

Tancred came up. Dave ran his eyes up and down Tancred's lean figure.

"How many people does this stage usually carry?"

Tancred shrugged. "It varies. Sometimes five or six, sometimes only one or two. Once in a while there aren't any passengers at all."

"Mail?"

"I take care of the horses here."

"But you've got eyes," snapped Dave. "You know what a mail pouch is, don't you?"

"I've seen them."

"All right, does the stage carry them?"

"Yes."

"Think carefully, now," said the squat man, wickedly. "Does she also carry a strong box?"

"No."

The outlaw grabbed the whiskey bottle from Jethro, took a great swig then passed it on to Dave. With a sudden spring he leaped forward and hit Tancred in the face with the back of his hand.

"I asked you about a strong box?"

"And I told you."

The short man rocked Tancred's head with a backhanded swipe. "What about a shotgun guard?"

"Don't do that again," Tancred said, evenly.

The little man took a step back. "Why, he's got spunk," he said, mockingly. "He might even try to fight me." He winked at Dave. "Shall we tell him who we are?"

Dave shrugged. "He's a horse-handler. He's probably never even heard of us."

"Everybody's heard of Sam Older," chortled the squat man. He pointed at Tancred. "Even you."

Tancred said in an even, flat tone, "Sam Older's dead."

"Sure, but Dick Small ain't." The short one tapped his chest. "Or Dave Helm." He indicated Dave.

Nine years ago Dick Small had been a thin man about six inches taller than the one who now called himself Dick Small. And Dave Helm . . . this man wasn't Dave Helm, not in a thousand years.

Tancred looked at Jethro. "And I suppose he's . . . Wes Tancred."

Jethro took that as a deadly insult. "Why, damn your

soul to hell, don't you accuse me of me being that dirty traitor. . . ."

Tancred backed away. "How was I to know? Seems to me, I heard men talking about the Older gang and the name Tancred. . . ."

"Don't mention Older and Tancred in the same breath," cried the man who called himself Dick Small. "Tancred was a scurvy rat who wormed his way into the gang, then shot Older when he wasn't looking."

"For ten thousand dollars blood money," added Dave.

"I'm just a horse-handler," Tancred said. He looked at Dave. "Like you said."

"See that you remember it," Dave retorted. "And you'd better tell the agent who we are. Just so he doesn't try another fool play, like with that rifle."

"We mean business," snapped Jethro.

Tancred nodded and started away but Dave grabbed his arm and whirled him around. "You didn't answer Dick's question—about the stage carrying a shotgun guard."

"I've never seen one," said Tancred. He waited a moment. "Can I go now?"

"Sure," said Dave. "As long as you stay in sight." He nodded toward the stage station. "And I don't mean in there."

Tancred went into the corral. He busied himself currying the stage horses, but every now and then he glanced toward the three outlaws. They had hunkered down outside the corral, near their own horses, and were killing the bottle of whiskey.

After a while they started a noisy three-handed poker game and kept at it until late afternoon, when they finally broke up the game and demanded food.

Tancred went to the stage station and stopped outside the door of the lean-to. Laura was working inside.

"They want something to eat," he said.

"I'm fixing it now," Laura replied. Tancred hesitated and was about to turn away when she said, "I saw them hit you."

Tancred let out a slow sigh. "Yes."

She gave him a quick look. "I'm sorry I said that."

"Why should you be sorry about it? They hit me all right."

"That isn't what I meant. I mean . . ." She was flustered

as she tried to straighten it out. "I shouldn't have said *anything* about it."

Vesser appeared in the lean-to, coming from inside the cabin.

"I hid the revolver, John."

Tancred frowned. "Two of them claim to be members of the old Sam Older gang . . . Dick Small and Dave Helm."

Vesser whistled. "Then there's no question about them holding up the stage!"

"No, I don't think so."

A yell came from the men by the corral. "Hey—how about that grub?"

"It's ready," Laura said.

Tancred relayed the information to the outlaws and they came toward the stage station, going in by the front door. Before Dave entered he signalled to Tancred to follow.

The supper consisted merely of beans and cornbread, but to the ruffians it was good fodder and they ate it with enthusiasm. Vesser sat at one end of the table, morosely eating his food without raising his eyes from the plate.

When they had finished eating, Dave looked toward the kitchen. "You got another bottle of whiskey out there?"

"You looked," Vesser said, curtly.

"Just in the kitchen. I didn't look in here."

"Then search."

"I may do just that." Dave got up. He looked around the room, but the effort of searching did not appeal to him. He shrugged and headed for the door. "Guess I'll roll in. We may not get much sleep tomorrow night."

He went out and after a moment Jethro and Dick followed. Tancred got up from the table and his eyes met Laura's. She said, "What are you going to do, John?"

"I'm going to sleep."

Her eyes fell from his. "Of course."

"They'll be watching me," Tancred said. "There isn't anything I can do."

Vesser said, "I thought maybe you could ride up the trail ten-fifteen miles and warn the stage."

"Make no mistake," Tancred said, soberly. "They're hard cases. Even if I could get a horse and get away they'd take it out on you and . . ." His eyes went to Laura.

"I've got the revolver," Vesser reminded.

"I wish you didn't have it." Tancred hesitated. "You've fired a gun, Mr. Vesser. And you've probably hit your target."

"I'm better with a rifle."

"You're not better than they are," Tancred said, earnestly. "There's a difference in shooting at a deer and—and a man. You have an aversion to killing—any normal man has—and whether you'd want to or not, you'd hesitate before actually pulling the trigger on a human being. They won't. They're killers. As a matter of fact they told me that they once rode with Sam Older."

"That riffraff!"

Tancred stopped. Sam Older was a legendary figure. Even to people like Vesser and his daughter. He was Robin Hood, of Robin Hood and his Merry Men.

There was nothing more for Wes Tancred to say. He exhaled slowly and started for the door.

"Wait, John," Vesser said. "I want to talk to you." He turned to Laura. "Do you mind leaving us alone, Laura?"

Laura minded, all right, but dutifully she went into the lean-to kitchen. Then Vesser said, "Believe me, John, I don't want to talk to you like this. But I've got to. I've thought of it all afternoon and I don't know which way to turn. I've got to *know* . . . about you and Laura."

A shudder ran through Tancred. "I'm sorry, Mr. Vesser," he said, "I can't answer that."

"I said this was going to be awkward and in the regular course of events wild horses couldn't make me talk like this. Only now . . . with those men out there . . . I've got to know."

"So you're going to fight them!"

"A man's got to do what he's got to do."

"Knowing that they'll kill you?"

"Even knowing that." A fine film of perspiration appeared on Vesser's forehead. "What is it, John . . . what is it about you that I can't grasp? I've watched you and I've studied you for six weeks. In any case, whether it's those men out there or not, I haven't got long. A matter of months, that's all. And I can't go without knowing about Laura. I'd hoped . . ."

"No!" said Tancred.

"Why not? Oh, I've seen her look at you and I've seen

you watching her. Then, why not, John, why not? Is it because you're already married?"

"No, it isn't that. I'm not married."

"Then, what is it?"

"I can't tell you."

"But I'm backed against a wall. You can tell me."

"I can't."

Vesser went around to attack the problem from the flank, as he'd probably done over and over in his mind. "You were sick when you came here, John, I know that. But I've watched you—you're better. I don't think it's that. You stopped here because it's an isolated spot. I've thought of that. Perhaps . . . you're wanted. . . "

"I'm not wanted."

A groan was torn from Vesser's throat. "Are you in love with Laura?"

The pain in Tancred's chest was as bad as it had ever been before he'd come out here to the Kansas prairie. But that was good. It was the shell Tancred knew so well. Behind it he was safe.

He said, "If I could be in love with any woman, I could be in love with Laura. But I'm not in love with her . . . because it isn't in me to love any person on earth."

Vesser capitulated. "All right, Bailey, all right, but I wish to God I had never set eyes on you!"

Tancred went out of the stage station and Laura came out of the lean-to where she had listened at the door and heard every word between her father and Tancred. She went into his arms and sobs wracked her body and Vesser wept.

Chapter 3

Morning came and Tancred came out of the shed where he had slept. The outlaws, two of them, were still sleeping beside the corral. The third, Jethro, was seated on the ground, his back to the corral poles, cleaning his gun with a dirty rag. As filthy as the three men were about their own persons, their guns were cleaned and well-oiled. Guns were the tools of their trade.

Over in the lean-to there was a clanking of pans as Laura prepared breakfast.

"That's a sweet morsel over there," Jethro observed to Tancred. "If I was a woman's man, I'd put my brand on that." He chuckled wickedly. "I'll bet you've already lit the fire under your branding iron."

"I've got work to do," said Tancred, heading for the corral gate.

Jethro sprang to his feet. "You're going to get those horses ready for the stage, just as if nothing was going to happen?"

"My job is feeding and watering and taking care of these horses." Tancred went into the corral.

When he came out the outlaws were all up and in the stage station, eating their breakfast. No one had called Tancred. He went into the shed and with a quick look over his shoulder, moved far in to the manger that was used by the horses during bad weather. It was half-filled with hay.

Tancred moved aside some of the hay and exposed a weathered carpetbag. He stared at it for a long moment, then shook his head and covered it again with hay.

When he went outside, Dave was coming out of the stage station. "Your breakfast's ready." He smacked his lips. "That girl cooks all right."

Tancred crossed the yard and entered the station. Dick

and Jethro were just finishing their breakfast, but Vesser sat at the plain table, his corncakes barely touched.

Tancred sat down opposite him and Laura brought him cakes and coffee. He ate and spoke no word to her or to her father and when he finished eating he went outside.

He curried the horses in the corral until their coats glistened. He rubbed them down with wisps of hay and curried them again. But at last he could work in the corral no longer and he came out.

The man who called himself Dave Helm looked at Tancred and said, "It's eating out your insides, isn't it? I don't know why it should. You're only a horse wrangler and the stage line shouldn't mean a damn thing to you."

"It doesn't."

"They can afford to lose anything we take from them." He looked thoughtfully toward the stage station.

Trancred went into the shed and threw himself upon the dirt floor. After a moment he heard a step and rolling his head to one side, saw Dave standing in the doorway, looking down on him.

"I just want to tell you that we mean business. If the old jasper over there don't know it by now, you'd better go and tell him."

"I've told him."

"Tell him again. No—I'll tell him myself."

Dave clumped away.

The outlaws had their dinner at twelve, but Tancred went without his. At one o'clock he got out the harness and got his six-horse team ready. A cloud of dust to the north told him that the stage was on time.

They saddled up their mounts, tied them to the top pole of the corral. Jethro climbed to the top of the corral and studied the approaching stage.

He climbed to the ground.

"Ten minutes."

Vesser came out of the stage station. His revolver was in his hand.

"Look!" said the squat man.

"Be damned!" exclaimed Dave.

Tancred cried out, "Throw down the gun . . . please?"

Vesser came toward the corral. Jethro edged over to the right, Dave to the left and Dick remained in the middle. Vesser was still seventy or seventy-five feet away and he thrust out his gun as he walked and fired.

The bullet missed Dick by three feet.

Dick's first bullet didn't miss. Nor did Jethro's or Dave's. Vesser's gun went off once more but the bullet went toward the sky. Laura was rushing out of the house, screaming and sobbing . . . and Dave walked toward her fallen father and put another bullet into him.

By that time, Tancred was in the shed. He swept aside the hay from the manger, scooped out the carpetbag and tore it open. He plunged in his hand and brought out a holster wrapped about a gun.

He did not bother with the holster. Uncoiling it, he gripped the naked Navy Colt and stepped to the door of the shed.

His eyes went straight ahead, saw Laura on her knees, sobbing over her father.

Dave was the first to see him. Shock hit him as he saw the gun in Tancred's hand. Dick, looking at Dave's face, wheeled.

Tancred fired at Dave. The distance was seventy-five feet, but Tancred's bullet caught Dave square in the fore-head. Then Tancred pivoted and fired at Dick, once. Jethro let out a scream of sheer terror. He fired, but the thing he had just seen, deprived him of . . . everything. His bullet went completely wild.

Tancred shot him down.

He did not look at the fallen men again. He went for-ward to Laura, who had rocked back to her heels. Her tear-stained face was taut, her eyes wild.

"I shouldn't have waited," he said. "But I . . . I couldn't . . . I couldn't fire the gun."

"Who are you?" whispered Laura in awe.

"My name," said Tancred, "is Wes Tancred. . . ."

"Tancred!" cried Laura, in shock. "The man who . . ."

"The man who killed Sam Older. Now, you know. . . ."

She continued to stare at him, hunkered back on her heels. Tancred turned and walked back into the shed. He put the revolver into the holster, wrapped the belt about it and put it back into the carpetbag. Carrying the bag he went out and picked the best of the outlaws' horses. He hooked the handle of the carpetbag over the saddle horn and swung up onto the horse.

When he turned it away from the corral, Laura was coming toward him.

"Wait, Wes, wait! You can't go now."

"I've got to," said Tancred. "The stage will be here in a few moments. Go with them."

"You can't go, Wes. Please. I'll go with you. I—I don't care who you are or what you've done. . . ."

"It's no use, Laura. I'm sorry. It—it wouldn't be fair to you. Wes Tancred is dead. He died nine years ago when he killed Sam Older. John Bailey is only a ghost. And a ghost is . . . nothing!"

He rode away from her and she watched him go.

Chapter 4

Abilene had its brief day as a boom town when the Texas cattle herds came to it, up the Chisholm Trail. Then the rails crept westward and Wichita had its day of glory and Ellsworth and Dodge City.

And then it was Sage City.

When Wes Tancred stepped off the Kansas & Western train at Sage City he looked to the north of the tracks and saw homes and shaded streets, a few stores; a town that looked like so many of the newer Midwestern villages. Then he turned and looked down South Street and saw a dozen saloons and gambling halls, a score of stores and shops, a street lined with hitchrails and churning with horses and wagons and humanity.

Trail town.

He stepped off the depot platform and started down the street. A cowboy came charging up the middle of the street on a cow pony, whooping and shooting at the sky and nobody on the wooden sidewalks paid any attention to him. A bleary-eyed man in Levi's, run-down-at-the-heels boots and huge Stetson reeled out of a saloon and took a header under the hitchrail into the dust of the street.

Tancred passed *Fugger's Mercantile Store*, the *Longhorn Saloon*, the *Sage City Hardware Company*, *McCoy's Saloon & Gambling Hall*, the *Boston Store*, the *Texas Saloon* and then he came to a two-story building with the sign, *Sage City Hotel*.

Tancred went into the hotel and a pimply-faced youth of about nineteen, who was polishing a brass spittoon behind the little counter, shoved a register toward him.

Tancred wrote the name John Bailey in the book, hesitated, then added, St. Louis, Mo. The youthful clerk studied the inscription.

"Two dollars. If you're going to stay a whole week it's ten."

"I'll take it by the day," Tancred said. He took out two dollars and dropped them on the counter.

The clerk studied a key rack and took down a key. "Number five. That's right in front."

Out on the street a gun banged twice. Tancred inclined his head.

"Doesn't Sage City have a marshal?"

"Oh, sure, we got a marshal and two deputies. We got a lot of laws around here."

Tancred picked up his carpetbag and valise and climbed the stairs to the second floor. He found that Room Number Five was the last door on the right. It was about nine by twelve in size, contained a cot, a washstand with a pitcher and bowl and a straight-backed chair. A row of nails on the wall served in lieu of a closet. The walls were rough wood, but painted with a single coat of paint.

Tancred took off his coat, poured water into the washbowl and washed his face and hands. Then he opened his valise and took out a clean shirt. He rolled up his soiled shirt and put it into the carpetbag. His hand touched a bundle at the bottom of the bag. He hesitated, then unrolled the bundle and exposed a well-oiled Navy Colt revolver. His face became bleak as he tested the gun, spinning the cylinder, trying the hammer and trigger, making sure that the cylinder was turned to the one empty chamber. Finally he re-wrapped the gun and put it back into the bottom of the carpetbag.

He put on his coat and descended to the lobby.

A sleepy-eyed man of about forty had taken over the desk. He was studying the ledger and did not seem very happy about it. "You're Mr. Bailey, the new guest?" he asked as Tancred came up.

"That's right."

"I'm the proprietor, Joe Handy. The boy gave you Number Five. I was saving that for Mr. Smith. Hong Kong Smith. He's checking in tomorrow." He looked inquiringly at Tancred. "Expect to stay here long?"

"That depends."

Joe Handy nodded. "Drummer?"

Tancred shook his head. "Can you tell me where I can find the *Sage City Star?*"

"Luke Miller's newspaper?" The hotel man frowned.

"You aren't, uh, going to work for Luke, are you?"

"That depends on him. He advertised for a man and —I'm looking for a job." Tancred looked shrewdly at Handy. "Anything wrong about that?"

"N-no, it isn't that. Only, well, Luke's got some of the people down on him. Not, me, though," Handy added hastily. "It's just, well, Luke's kinda outspoken."

"A lot of newspapermen are."

"It don't make them popular, though." The hotel man drummed his fingers on the desk. "Luke's place is right around the corner on River Street. You can't miss it."

"Thanks."

Tancred nodded and left the hotel. Outside he walked to the cross street and turned right. Then he saw the sign: *Sage City Star, Luke Miller, Editor and Publisher. Job Printing.*

Inside was a desk, heaped with newspapers and papers, and in the rear, a large two-page newspaper press, two job presses and several typecases. An elderly man was setting up type and Luke Miller was fussing and fuming over the newspaper press, his face dabbed with ink, his hands black to the elbows with the stuff.

He looked up as Tancred entered.

"Be with you in a minute," he called.

Tancred walked back to him. "My weekly repair job," Miller complained. "This newfangled machinery they been making since the war just don't stand up. Always something going out of whack." He picked up a benzine-soaked rag and wiped his hands. "What can I do for you?"

"You had an ad in the *Publisher's Auxiliary*," Tancred said.

Miller's eyes lit up. "You're a printer?" He thrust out his blackened hand and grabbed Tancred's. "Never thought a man'd come out here to this jumping off place!"

"You're here."

"That's because I haven't got any sense. How much pay do you want?"

"I'll leave that to you."

Miller winced. "Don't do that. I'll take advantage of you." He strode past Tancred to the littered desk and scooped up a copy of the *Sage City Star*. "Here's last week's sheet. Thirty dollars' worth of advertising in it."

"That doesn't seem like much."

"It isn't." Miller paused. "I may as well tell you the

rest. There's a boycott against me in town among the merchants. They don't like the things I write for the paper."

He exclaimed and held up his index finger. Tancred heard a burst of gunfire on South Street. "That's what I'm fighting."

"You mean there are people who approve of that?"

"Jacob Fugger approves of it. He approves of anything the Texas men want to do."

"I saw Fugger's name on a store," Tancred said.

"There's a lot of stores you didn't see it on," Miller exclaimed. "Places he owns or has an interest in. The bank for instance." Miller bared his teeth. "Fugger's our local tycoon, in addition to being the mayor of Sage City. In other words, he runs the town. That's why I'm carrying thirty dollars' worth of advertising instead of three hundred. And it's also the reason I'm doing twenty to thirty dollars' worth of job printing a week instead of a couple of hundred. And that's why I can't pay you more than twenty dollars a week."

"I don't see how you can afford to pay even that much."

"Well, there's some money comes in from subscriptions and sales of the paper. The people like the Star, even if the businessmen don't." Miller looked at Tancred. "I've told you the worst. Do you want the job?"

"When do I start?"

"Right now, if you want to. We go to press tomorrow and we're behind. Mose . . . !" He turned and called to the elderly printer. "Mose, this is our new man, Mr.—?"

"John Bailey," Tancred said, quickly.

"John Bailey, Mose Hudkins."

Tancred shook hands with the old printer. "A cousin of mine has a shop back in Sterling, Illinois," Hudkins said. "He had a man named Bailey working for him a couple of years ago. Young fellow."

Tancred shook his head. "I never worked in Sterling."

"This man's name wasn't John, though, as I recall. Thought you might be related to him."

"I have no relatives in the printing business."

"I've got one," declared Miller. "My wife. She's been helping out on Tuesdays and Wednesdays. That reminds me, Bailey, you'll need a place to live."

"I checked in at the hotel."

"You won't get much sleep there. Not with the Texas men in town."

"The proprietor wants my room tomorrow. A special guest. Mr. Hong Kong Smith."

Miller grimaced. "The grand Mr. Hong Kong Smith! So, he's to be with us again. One of the leading citizens of Texas. Brings up a half-dozen herds every season, but he doesn't come with the herds himself. Too rough for him. Takes a boat to New Orleans, then a steamer up the river to St. Louis and then from St. Louis to here by way of the Kansas & Western. Mr. Smith's a very popular man—in Texas. He brings northern gold to Texas. Pays five dollars per steer on the hoof and sells it here in Kansas for thirty dollars."

"Odd name for a cattleman," Tancred observed.

"He was a clipper-ship man before the war. Made a pile trading with the Orient. At least that's the story he's spread about himself. My personal opinion is that he made his money as a slaver, running slaves from Africa." Miller drew in a deep breath. "But he's quite a man, Mr. Hong Kong Smith. And so are the Texas men who bring his herds up the trail."

"If you have no objection," Tancred said, "I could put up a cot back here in the shop."

"I've no objection. I only wish I could put you up at the house. But we just don't have the room. And during the cattle season it's almost impossible to find a place in town. I'll stop in at the Boston Store this afternoon and have them send over a cot and some blankets."

"That'll be fine, Mr. Miller. And now I might as well get familiar with the typecases."

"You'll find some copy on the hooks. The big one's got straight matter, the small one ads."

Tancred took off his coat, hung it on a nail and walked to the typecases. Without hesitation he reached for a sheet of copy on the smaller hook. Miller, watching covertly, smiled.

An hour later, when Mose came to him, the newspaper owner said, softly, "I think we've got a printer, Mose!"

Chapter 5

Tancred left the newspaper shop a little after six and went to his hotel where he washed up. Coming down from his room he stood in front of the hotel a few minutes, then crossed the street to the Bon Ton restaurant and had a supper of fried steak and potatoes.

When he came out the street was more crowded than it had been during the day. More horses were tied to the hitchrails. He crossed to the hotel and went up to his room. It was stifling in the confined place. He opened a window and the street noises assailed his ears.

Up the street a cowboy yipped and emptied his revolver. The shooting was repeated by someone at the other end of the street. There would be no early sleep for the guests of the hotel.

He descended again to the hotel lobby and standing by the door watched the traffic on the street for a few minutes. Finally he went out. He strolled to the depot, stood there for a while, then returned to the hotel.

The tinkly music of a piano from the Texas Saloon next door caught his attention and on a sudden impulse he turned and went to the saloon and entered.

Although it was scarcely seven o'clock the place was crowded. A bar ran down half of one side of the room and the entire front section was given over to tables and various games of chance. A crowd stood around the main faro table.

At the rear of the room was a small raised platform on which stood a piano. A bleary-eyed oldster sat at the instrument, playing a fast tune.

Tancred found a spot at the far end of the bar and ordered a glass of beer from one of the four bartenders. He put the glass to his mouth and the piano player suddenly switched from his fast piece to a ballad.

Tancred drank some of his beer, but he did not taste

25

it. A girl began singing and he turned and looked toward the stage at the rear of the room.

She was in her early twenties, and wore a low-cut velvet gown. A beautiful girl with a fine voice. She sang her song and she sang it well. Tancred had heard it so many times during the past nine years but he had seldom heard it sung better.

The ballad was the saga of Sam Older and the man who had killed him. The words were mawkish and there was little truth in them. They told of a bold man who had been forced to become an outlaw, a man who stole and yes, who killed, but who did those things only from lofty motives. His wealth he gave to the poor, his gun was used only on behalf of the persecuted and the downtrodden. He righted wrongs. He was a fine man, Sam Older, and his men were loyal and true . . . save for the cowardly Wes, the youth befriended by Sam Older, who betrayed him for gold and laid him low by a shot in the back. The ballad of Sam Older ended with the verse, but the chorus, repeated, was the saga of Wes Tancred . . . Tancred, the outcast, the man shunned by all men righteous and true . . . the coward . . . the traitor, the murderer who would meet his end alone and cravenly and mourned by none.

Tancred had heard the song a thousand times, in cow camps, in railroad camps, deep down in mines. In towns and villages, in theaters and in saloons, on the streets and in houses.

He heard it now in the Texas Saloon, in Sage City, Kansas.

The girl finished the song and the applause was thunderous. She left the stage and was pawed by a Texas man or two, but she coolly brushed away their hands and worked her way through the crowds to the bar.

Tancred saw now that she had gorgeously golden hair, a smooth, fine complexion . . . and tired eyes of the palest blue.

She said to Tancred, "Your beer's gone flat. Have another." She signalled to the bartender. "Give the gentleman a fresh glass, Chippy."

Tancred nodded. "Can I buy you a drink?"

"You don't have to. I own the place."

"I'll still buy you a drink."

"Why? You didn't like my singing."

"I thought you sang very well."

"I was looking at you when I finished. You were the only man in ths place who didn't applaud."

"I've heard the song before."

"Who hasn't? But they still want it." She looked at him thoughtfully. "You're not a Texas man."

He shook his head.

"Gambler?"

"Printer."

"You work for Luke Miller?"

"You said that just like the hotel man," Tancred said.

"Miller's trying to put us out of business."

"He's a newspaperman and a newspaperman's job is to print the truth."

"What's the truth? Luke Miller wants to clean up Sage City. From his point of view that's probably the right thing. But I run a saloon. So do a lot of other people in this town. The saloon-keepers want an everything-goes town." The proprietress of the Texas Saloon smiled at Tancred. "You see, it all depends on where you stand. What's good for one isn't good for another. By the way, my name is Lily Leeds. It used to be Maggie Leeds, but Lily sounds better than Maggie."

"My name is Bailey."

A lean, sardonic-eyed man at Tancred's left turned. "Bailey, did you say? He wore a badge on which was the word, "Marshal."

"Mr. Bailey," Lily Leeds said, "Marshal Lee Kinnaird."

The marshal nodded, his eyes full on Tancred's face. "That wouldn't be John Bailey?"

"Why, yes."

"You worked for the stage line at Turkey Crossing?"

Tancred hesitated, then nodded.

Marshal Kinnaird gave a low whistle. "I got a Wichita paper yesterday. It had a piece about you."

"Is it true?" exclaimed Lily. She made a small gesture. "People have been talking about it."

"I haven't seen the paper, so I don't know what it said."

The marshal pursed up his lips. "It said that three men killed Vesser, the station agent. It also said that the horse wrangler then killed said three men." The marshal paused. "With exactly three shots."

"That's shooting," said Lily. "And you're a printer now?"

"I've been a printer for quite a few years," said Tancred. "The job at Turkey Crossing was only a temporary one. Until last week I hadn't fired a gun in quite a while."

"Yet you downed three bad men with just three bullets," said the marshal.

"It was just one of those things."

"Was it?" Kinnaird frowned. "Bailey, John Bailey. I never heard the name before."

"Mr. Bailey," Lily said. "I'll buy you a drink."

"And I'll drink with you," declared Kinnaird.

Lily signalled to the bartender. "Chippy, drinks for Mr. Bailey and the marshal."

"A beer," said Tancred.

"Beer!" cried Lily.

Kinnaird smiled crookedly. "I think *I'll* have a beer."

Lily shook her head. "I won't. Beer's fattening."

The bartender brought the beers for the men and a small glass for Lily. It contained a liquid that looked like whiskey but was actually cold tea.

The marshal raised his glass to Tancred. "John Bailey." He quaffed some of the beer. "A printer."

"Who works for Luke Miller," Lily added.

Kinnaird grinned. "I'm still drinking."

"You're against Miller?" Tancred asked.

"The mayor hired me and he can fire me. And who do you think is the mayor of Sage City?"

"Jacob Fugger," said Lily.

The marshal looked covertly over his shoulder. "Jacob Fugger, who owns Sage City."

"He doesn't own the Texas Saloon," said Lily.

"But you're not on Miller's side," Tancred reminded.

"I'm on *my* side," Lily retorted.

Chapter 6

Jacob Fugger added the last digit in the column of figures and wrote down the sum. He looked at it a moment and pleasure seeped through him. The gross volume of his store had been very good, the lumberyard had sold an unusually large amount of lumber, the bank deposits were at an all-time high and two of three businesses that had rather substantial loans had made their payments and the third had met its interest payment. The hideyard had two hundred thousand buffalo hides ready for shipment and there were four carloads of buffalo bones on the siding and enough bones to fill up three more cars.

Business was good and Hong Kong Smith's first trail herd of the season had arrived. Much of the money that would be paid to Hong Kong Smith would find its way eventually into Fugger's hands, through one or another of the channels that Fugger owned or controlled.

There was only one fly in Jacob Fugger's ointment and he thought about it as he scanned the figures that told of the success of his numerous enterprises. Ten years ago, at the age of 45, Fugger had been a clerk in a dry-goods store, back in a small Ohio town. All he had had to look forward to was another twenty or thirty years of drudgery, the accumulation of a paltry few dollars every year by personal scrimping.

He was a withering, aging man at 45, without hope. And then, one night, there had been a burglary at the store. Five hundred dollars in cash had been taken. Fugger was not suspected of course. He had been at the store too long.

Yet a month later, Fugger left Ohio. He took the cars to St. Louis and then to Kansas City. He arrived there just as the first shipment of Texas longhorns was received at the stockyards. He learned that these steers had been driven north from Texas to the new railroad that was being built across the state of Kansas. The tracks were then at a little place called Abilene.

Fugger went to Abilene and for five hundred dollars bought a quarter interest in a small store. A year later he was the sole owner of the store in Abilene and since the railroad had gone on another hundred miles to the west, Fugger established a new store at the terminus.

Five years and five stores later, Fugger arrived in Sage City. From here the railroad headed due west, into Colorado. This was the closest it would ever come to Texas and here, Fugger decided, would be his last stand. Eventually, someone would build a railroad down into Texas, but that would not be for another few years and by that time Fugger would not care.

Heavy feet clomped up the stairs to the porch over the rear of the big store where Fugger did his bookkeeping. The huge head of Bill Bleek appeared.

"Van Meter's here," Bleek said, shortly.

"Send him up. There'll be some others, too. Let them in as they come, but don't let anyone else in the store."

"Just the usual?"

Fugger nodded. Bill Bleek stomped down the stairs and after a moment Van Meter came up. He was about forty, a smooth-looking man in Prince Albert and well-brushed derby.

"It's seven o'clock," he said.

"The rest'll be here in a few minutes."

"What's it about?"

"Hong Kong Smith's arriving in town tomorrow."

Van Meter nodded. "I thought he was due. His trail herd arrived yesterday."

"You've the money ready for him?"

"We've enough."

"He'll be paying his men. You know what that means?"

Van Meter grimaced. "We won't be getting much sleep. Unless . . ."

Fugger shook his head. "The money might as well stay in Sage City."

"It usually does."

"It won't if Luke Miller has much more to say. Smith can drive his herds to Ellsworth or to Dodge without much more trouble. And if he goes to one of the other towns, the Texas men will follow him."

A step sounded on the steps leading up to the veranda

and Fugger made a small gesture to the banker. The broad, placid face of Morgan Holt, the hardware man, appeared.

"Evening, Jacob," he said. "Hello, Horace."

"Thanks for stopping by, Morgan."

"It's no trouble. We're having a late dinner."

More steps creaked on the stairs and two men came up, Packard, the owner of the Boston Store and McCoy, who owned the biggest saloon in Sage City and had money in one or two other enterprises. Close on their heels came a pudgy man of about fifty, who wore a floppy black hat, a soiled white shirt and a long string tie. This was Judge Olsen.

Fugger then rolled out the ball. "I called you here to talk about Luke Miller."

"That's what I thought it would be about," remarked Packard.

Fugger regarded Packard without pleasure. "Perhaps I shouldn't have asked you."

Packard shrugged. "I can leave."

"And have you say we're all scheming behind your back?" Fugger snapped. "Stay. I'll say what I've got to say. It's been a long winter and we've got a short season ahead of us. Four good months, maybe five. We're businessmen and we've got to make the most of those few months."

"Amen!" exclaimed McCoy, the saloon man.

"The point is," continued Fugger, "what are we going to do about Luke Miller and his newspaper?"

"I don't see that we can do anything," declared Packard. "Luke's got a right to put out a newspaper."

"He hasn't got a right to slander anyone," retorted Fugger. He pointed to the judge. "Isn't that so, Judge?"

Judge Olsen cleared his throat. "A newspaper can't libel a citizen."

"Is the truth libel?" asked Packard.

"I think," said Jacob Fugger, "we can do without you."

Packard drew a deep breath and let it out heavily. "I think you can. But before I go, I want to say a few words."

"You don't have to."

"But I'm going to. I came to Sage City four years ago because I was looking for a new town, where I could settle down with my family. I brought money to this town and I've made money here. I've built a home and for five months of the year my wife is afraid to step out of the house and I can't let my children on the street, for the fear of a wild cowboy riding or shooting them down. Sure, we've made money from the Texas men, but we could have made it without them. The land that the Texas cattle trample with their hoofs is the finest farming land in the state. Farmers have come in and more would come if they could settle down in peace. The future of this area, as I see it, is not with the Texas cattle drovers, but with Kansas farmers. . . ."

"Are you finished, Mr. Packard?" Fugger asked coldly.

"No, but I can see that I'm wasting my breath. Good evening, gentlemen."

Packard stepped to the stairs and descended them.

"And now," said Fugger, heavily, "we'll get on with the business. Judge, how much did you make on fines last year?"

Judge Olsen squirmed. "Barely enough to get by."

"You made," said Fugger, "six thousand, two hundred and forty-five dollars. Most of that money came from the Texas men."

"I fine them as they come. The marshal and his men arrest them."

"They're not going to arrest as many men this year."

The judge showed great displeasure. "But my office is a fee office. There's no salary connected with it."

"We'll have to make other arrangements. The marshal and his men can't arrest people for every trivial violation of the city ordinances. A man has a right to enjoy himself in our town. We'll let that word get around among the Texas men and we'll have more herds coming here than all the other trail towns put together."

"And what about Luke Miller?" put in McCoy, the saloon man.

"He's got to be taken care of."

"How?"

"Leave that to me."

Morgan Holt cleared his throat. "Within reason, Jacob. You're the mayor and we're the city council, but remember we've got an election in a little while. And Miller's paper gets to the people who vote."

"It may not be reaching them by election day."

Chapter 7

The noise of the Texas men carousing and brawling went on long after midnight and it was two o'clock before Wes Tancred fell asleep, but he was up shortly after six and by seven o'clock he was having his breakfast.

The waitress looked at him curiously but she waited until he was eating before she spoke of what was on her mind.

"You're John Bailey, aren't you?" she asked then.

"Why, yes."

"Is it true that you backed down Wyatt Earp, in Dodge?"

"Who's been saying that?" exclaimed Tancred. "I've never even met Wyatt Earp."

"Why, everybody in town's talking about you. How you wiped out that band of outlaws, singlehanded."

Tancred groaned. He hastened through his breakfast and went down to the print shop. As early as it was both Hudkins and Miller were already on the job. And they had heard about John Bailey. Miller had a copy of the Wichita paper in his hand as Tancred came into the shop.

"This true?" he asked.

Tancred took the paper from Miller and skimmed through the piece about the Turkey Crossing affair. It was a lurid account, as told by the driver of the stagecoach and the passengers who hadn't actually seen what happened, but who had seen the evidence and had received additional information from the hysterical surviving witness whose father had been murdered by the men whom retribution had overtaken so swiftly.

Tancred handed back the paper to Miller. "They didn't get this from me."

"But it's essentially true?"

"I worked for Vesser, the agent at Turkey Crossing until last week."

"You were a hostler?"

"I wanted to work outdoors for a while."

"Sick?"

"I was. I'm better now."

Miller looked thoughtfully at Tancred. "Is John Bailey your real name?"

"Does it matter?"

"You're a printer. As long as you can set up type your name could be Benjamin Franklin. Or Johannes Gutenberg. Only—"

"Yes?"

"Nothing." Miller got up and nodded to the rear of the shop. "I had your cot set up. Why don't you get your things from the hotel and move in?"

"I believe I will. They want my room for Hong Kong Smith."

Tancred nodded and left the print shop. He rounded the corner and strode to the hotel. As he reached it he remembered that there had been no soap in the hotel and decided to buy some. He was about to cross to the Boston Store, then saw the sign of the Fugger Store.

He was curious to see Jacob Fugger, who loomed so importantly in the affairs of Sage City.

He entered the store, saw a middle-aged woman behind the notions counter. He swerved away from it to go to the rear where he saw shelves of groceries. And then he stopped. Behind a counter containing clothing was Laura Vesser. He moved toward her.

"I didn't expect to see you here."

Her eyes were steady, but impassive. "I've been here for a week."

"Why Sage City? I thought you'd be going east."

"I've nothing in the east." She paused. "I heard you were here."

"I'm working at the print shop. I was a printer before I came to Turkey Crossing."

"It's a job. Like this one." The casual indifference in her tone caused him to look at her sharply. She said, "Is there anything I can do for you?"

He shook his head.

"If you need anything, Mr. Bailey," she went on, emphasizing the name, "Fugger's Store has it. Everything from shirts to shoes, groceries to—guns."

He nodded and walked stiffly out of the store.

Joe Handy was talking to a lean, swarthy man in the

hotel when Tancred entered. They stopped talking and both watched him as he climbed the stairs to the second floor.

It took him only a moment to get his things together and he descended to the lobby. The swarthy man was still at the desk.

"You can have the room now for Hong Kong Smith," Tancred told Handy.

The hotel man grimaced. "I can fix you up with another room, Mr. Bailey. Something just about as good."

"I've found another place."

"Sorry to hear that. I'd been proud to have you stay. Oh—Mr. Bailey, shake hands with Chuck Gorey. Chuck's one of our deputy marshals."

Gorey's hand was flaccid and clammy, entirely free of calluses. It was the hand of a professional gunfighter.

"How're you?" Tancred said.

"Good to find," replied Gorey, his pale eyes regarding Tancred appraisingly. "So you're the lad wiped out those bad men over at Turkey Crossing?"

Tancred made an impatient gesture. "Time I got to work."

"I'll walk with you a piece."

Tancred was not pleased but the deputy fell in beside him. As they came out of the hotel Gorey said softly, "I didn't think Miller had it in him."

Tancred looked at him sidewards. "What do you mean?"

Gorey grinned. "They *have* been pushing him around. Can't say's I blame him for sending for you."

"I'm working for Mr. Miller as a printer," Tancred said, coldly.

"Sure, sure."

"That's the truth, Gorey."

"Chuck, to my friends."

"Luke Miller hired me—as a printer—before he even heard of the Turkey Crossing thing."

"All *right*, Bailey."

A gun banged up the street. It was followed by a veritable thunder of gunfire, punctuated by the whooping of a score of men.

"The train's in," said the deputy. "That'll be Mr. Hong Kong Smith's boys welcoming him." He chuckled. "Now the old town will liven up." He gave Tancred a half salute and turning headed back up the street toward the depot.

Tancred continued on to the print shop. Packard, the owner of the Boston Store, was leaving as he came in. A frown creased Luke Miller's forehead.

"Fugger's declared war," Miller said. "He called a meeting of the city council last night. From now on Sage City's an open town. Packard tried to talk against it and Fugger ran him out of the meeting." He winced as the thunder of gunfire on South Street came over.

"Hong Kong Smith's arrived in town," Tancred said.

Chapter 8

Hong Kong Smith towered well above six feet six in his high-heeled boots. He was about forty-five, tipped the scales at two hundred and seventy and down in Texas they said that you could hear his voice about as far as the ball of a needle gun would carry.

He came out of the Sage City Bank, his huge hat filled with coin. The score of Texas men who had brought the first trail herd of the season up the Chisholm Trail let out a roar. About a dozen fired their guns.

Hong Kong Smith shouted the Texas men into silence. "Come and get it, you dirty, mangy sons of Texas!"

He led the way across the street to the Texas Saloon, set the hatful of money on the bar. "Whiskey!" he roared. "Bring whiskey!"

A bartender brought a bottle and a couple of small glasses. "I said whiskey!" boomed Hong Kong, "and you call those glasses for men? These are Texas men!" He brushed the whiskey glasses off the bar.

A second bartender hurried up with two more bottles of whiskey and a water tumbler.

"That's more like it," growled Smith. He poured out a tumblerful of whiskey. "Let's do this businesslike. Who's first, beginning with A?"

"Adams," cried out a cowboy. "That's me."

"Adams," said Smith. "Forty-two dollars." He fished around in the hat, brought out four gold eagles and added two silver dollars. "Here's your money and—" He picked up the tumblerful of whiskey. "And this!"

The Texas man winced but drained off the huge amount of whiskey. He sputtered and choked and Hong Kong Smith slapped him on the back.

"Next man," he sang out.

"Baker," cried a Texas man.

Smith refilled the big glass of whiskey and forced it

on the man called Baker. He paid him his forty-two dollars, booming out, "You don't spend any of that. Not today, you don't. Today Hong Kong Smith pays the bill."

"Hooray for Hong Kong Smith!" yelled a man and the ovation was taken up by every Texas man in the Texas Saloon.

Lily Leeds came out of her office. Hong Kong Smith whooped when he saw her. "Lily, my girl, you get prettier every time I see you."

"Oh, it's you again," said Lily in disgust. "I should have known."

"That's what I like about you—your sense of humor," roared Smith. He swooped Lily into his arms. "Give us a kiss, Lily girl."

She slapped his face, but the big man crushed her to him and forced her face up. He kissed her resoundingly and when he released her, she rocked his head with hard slaps. But Smith was impervious.

"Whiskey," he roared. "Whiskey for everyone in the house. Hong Kong Smith pays the bill."

A half hour later every Texas man in Sage City was drunk. They smashed four tables in the Texas Saloon and broke the back-bar mirror. Then, with Smith in the lead, they moved to McCoy's Saloon and pretty well wrecked that.

By noon a half dozen of Hong Kong's men had fallen by the wayside, but the rest carried on. The only difference was that they were no longer in one group. A few men were bucking the faro games about town, some kept on with the drinking but had drifted to various saloons, one or two here, two or three there.

Marshal Kinnaird and his deputies, acting upon instructions from Mayor Fugger, discreetly stayed out of the way of the brawling men from Texas.

Chapter 9

Shortly before twelve Luke Miller brought a couple of sheets of copy paper to Tancred.

"Read that."

Tancred's eyes skimmed over the story, which bore the head, *The Devil and Texas Rule Sage City*. It was a strong piece, Luke Miller pulled no punches. Jacob Fugger, he said, catered to the lawless Texas men, because they were making him rich. The Kansas & Western Railroad paid him one dollar for every Texas steer that was shipped from Sage City. Through his bank, Fugger saw that the Texas Cowboys received hard cash in Sage City, instead of at their homes in Texas. And through his stores and saloons, Fugger saw that that money was taken away from them.

Fugger owned Sage City and he pulled the strings the way they suited him. Right now it suited him to let the Texas men run wild and the citizens of Sage City could expect only violence and bloodshed. The law would not curb the Texas men because Fugger owned the law.

Right now, if you were a Texas man and it suited you to insult a Sage City woman on the streets, that was perfectly all right. If you felt like breaking a few windows about town, no one would punish you for indulging your whim. Or, maybe your fancy ran to riding your horse on the sidewalks or into stores. Go right ahead, no one would stop you. As long as you paid your tribute to Jacob Fugger.

"What do you think?" Miller asked when Tancred finished reading the editorial.

"I'll set it up."

"After lunch will be all right . . . Fugger will never forgive me for that."

"He's not exactly your friend right now."

"Now he'll really put on the screws. But there's an

election in a month. My only chance is to try to rouse the local voters enough so they'll vote Fugger and his clique out of office. If they don't, I'm through in Sage City."

Tancred washed his hands and left the shop. He walked to South Street and crossed to go to the Bon Ton Café. As he walked along he heard angry yelling in McCoy's Saloon, then two quick shots.

A man catapulted out of McCoy's and made for the horses at the hitchrail. He mounted one and galloped up the street, emptying his revolver at the blue sky.

Tancred entered the Bon Ton Café and seated himself on a stool beside a giant of a man. Bill Bleek.

The waitress came up. "Hello, Mr. Bailey. What'll it be?"

"What've you got besides steak?"

"Steak."

"Then make it steak."

The girl went off and Bill Bleek turned to Bailey.

"Like Sage City?" he asked.

"A town's a town."

"Most people don't like Sage City," Bleek went on. "Too rough. Stranger in town got his teeth knocked out last week. Some broken ribs, too."

"I mind my own business," Tancred said.

"Like at Turkey Crossing?"

Tancred looked sharply at Bleek. "Who knocked out this stranger's teeth?"

"Me."

"That's what I thought."

"Bill Bleek is the handle. I work for Jacob Fugger."

"And I work for Luke Miller."

"That's why I'm talking to you. You got a good set of teeth and there ain't no dentist in Sage City."

"I won't be needing one," Tancred said with restraint. "Miller's paying me as a printer."

Lee Kinnaird came in from the street. He frowned as he saw Bill Bleek, but he quickly erased the frown.

"One of your Texas friends just killed a faro dealer over at McCoy's."

"So?"

"I thought Fugger might want to know."

"You're the marshal, ain't you?"

"Uh-uh, not any more I'm not."

"Since when?"

"Since about two minutes ago."

"Jacob know?"

"I'm telling you to tell him."

"Tell him yourself."

Bill Bleek looked at Kinnaird thoughtfully. Then he got up from the stool. "Well, since you ain't the marshal any more . . ."

He suddenly hit Kinnaird in the face, a savage backhanded blow that knocked Kinnaird backward over a table.

Kinnaird got to his feet, blood dribbling from his mouth. "Where's your gun, Bleek?" he cried.

"You know I don't carry one."

"Then get one."

Bleek regarded Kinnaird impassively. "So you can gun me? Uh-uh, I'll fight any man living with my fists, but I'm no gunslinger." His eye flickered to Tancred. "Hear that, Bailey?"

"I heard it."

"Lay a hand on me again, Bleek," said Kinnaird ominously, "and gun or no gun, I'll kill you."

"Get out of town, Kinnaird," sneered Bleek. "If you ain't working for Jacob, you're against him."

Bleek swaggered out of the restaurant. Kinnaird dabbed at the blood on his chin. "You saw that, Bailey," he said. "What do you think of it now?"

"When I get back to the shop, I'm setting up an editorial that I think expresses it very well." Tancred paused. "The title is, *'The Devil and Texas Rule Sage City.'*"

"Does the piece give the name of the Devil?"

"Jacob Fugger."

Kinnaird whistled. "I think I quit my job just in time!"

"What about the deputies?"

"Slattery's a Texas man himself. Only he can't go back to Texas because a couple of sheriffs want him. Chuck Gorey . . ." Kinnaird shrugged. "He says he talked to you this morning."

"Yes, he did."

"Is it true, what he said?"

"No."

"Sorry to hear that. I was kind of wishing it was true. But the Turkey Crossing thing—*that* was true?" The ex-marshal watched Tancred's face closely. "I'm not the marshal any more."

"They killed Vesser, the agent, in cold blood. I—I caught them by surprise."

"Three against one?"

"They weren't expecting it."

Kinnaird shook his head slowly. "I have a strange notion, Bailey—that I'd rather fight Bill Bleek's fists than go up against you with a gun."

"I'm a printer, Kinnaird," Tancred said doggedly.

Jacob Fugger entered McCoy's Saloon and bore down on Hong Kong Smith who was leaning heavily against the bar. Fugger did not glance in the direction of the faro table, where the dealer lay on the floor.

"Smith," Fugger snapped. "What's the name of the cowboy who shot Thatcher?"

"Who's Thatcher?" Hong Kong Smith asked thickly.

"The faro dealer." Fugger gestured toward the table.

"Oh, him," said Smith. "Never saw him before."

"He's Thatcher," gritted Fugger. "I asked you the name of the cowboy who killed him."

Smith became drunkenly cagy. "What do you wanna know for?"

"So he can be arrested."

"Nobody's going to arrest any of my men."

"This man's going to be. He's got to be, Smith. He killed a man."

"Self-defense. It was self-defense."

"All right, then he'll be acquitted. But he's got to stand trial. I go along with you, Smith. I go along with you pretty far, but I can't go along with you on killing. He's got to stand trial."

But Hong Kong Smith still shook his head. "Harpending won't stand trial, Fugger. He's a high-spirited man and he won't—"

"Is this Manny Harpending you're talking about?"

"One of the best boys in Texas, when he isn't loaded with whiskey. That's what got him in trouble at home."

"The story is that he killed two men in Texas," snapped Fugger. "And what about that marshal over in Newton, two years ago?"

"He tried to buffalo Manny and Manny's a high-spirited boy—"

"You said that. But I still say he's got to give himself up."

"He won't."

"Then he's got to be arrested." Fugger held up his hand. "There were witnesses—*you* were a witness, weren't you?"

"Yes, of course. I saw Manny—"

"All right, you saw the whole thing. You saw Harpending draw in self-defense . . ."

Hong Kong Smith suddenly guffawed. "Yes sir, I sure saw it. Manny shot the dealer in self-defense, that's what he did."

A gun banged outside the saloon and the batwing doors burst open. Chuck Gorey, gun in hand, plunged into the room. He saw Jacob Fugger and came over.

"Here you are, Mr. Fugger. What're the rules if a Texas man tries to kill you?"

A bullet tore through the flimsy batwing doors and crashed into the bar. Outside a raucous voice yelled, "Come on out and fight, you goddam Yank!"

"That's what I mean," said Gorey.

"That's Harpending's voice!" boomed Hong Kong Smith.

"Arrest him," snapped Fugger.

Gorey looked at him blankly. "Arrest him, did you say?"

"Yes. Disarm and lock him up."

A shudder ran through Gorey. "He's got a six-shooter and a rifle and he's fighting drunk. . . ."

Hong Kong Smith roared. "That's all right, Marshal, Harpending won't hurt you. Not much. You just go out there and take away his guns and tell him to march down to the calaboose, nice and quiet."

"Come on out, you goddam marshal!" yelled Harpending out on the street.

"Yeah, come on out and dance," cried a second voice. "We got the music for you. Listen!" A bullet came zinging through the door, then a couple more.

Gorey darted to the side of the door and risked a quick peek out upon the street. He turned back. "He's got some Texas men with him."

"You've got to talk to him," Fugger cried to Hong Kong Smith.

"Talk to him yourself," declared Smith.

"He's your man. He works for you."

"That don't mean a thing," retorted Smith. "He works for me on the trail, not here in Kansas. And even when he's working for you, you don't go up to a man like Harpending when he's roaring drunk and has just killed a man and ask him to give you his gun, pretty please. I'm Hong Kong Smith and I'm alive and prosperous today because I know how to get along with Texas men. I know *when* to get along with them."

Fugger gave Smith a withering look and went over to Gorey. "Now, look here, Gorey. Kinnaird quit when the shooting started. That puts you in line for his job. You go out there and arrest that man and you get Kinnaird's job. Otherwise, you can quit, too."

Gorey looked toward the door. "I'll go out there and kill him. I'm not afraid of any man alive—"

"You can't kill him. You've got to take him alive."

Gorey stared at Fugger. "You drive a hard bargain, Mr. Fugger." He bit his lower lip. "The marshal's job pays three hundred a month, doesn't it?"

Fugger nodded. "That's a lot of money."

Gorey hitched up his cartridge belt, drew a deep breath and started for the door. He faltered as his hand reached for the batwings, but he went through.

Harpending and three Texas men were on their horses, across the street from McCoy's Saloon. Their height gave them a clear view over the horses tied to the hitchrail in front of the saloon.

Gorey popped out of the saloon, throwing up his left hand. "Hold your fire!" he cried out. "I want to talk to you."

Harpending whipped his rifle toward Gorey and fired. The bullet tore through the brim of Gorey's hat.

Gorey waited for no more. He whirled and plunged back into shelter. Before he disappeared a bullet from one of the other Texas men took off the left heel of his boot.

Harpending and his friends were now the rulers of Sage City. They yipped and whooped and fired their guns at random, crashing a store window here and there.

Then Harpending decided to pay a visit to Jacob Fugger. He assumed that he would find him in the latter's store and rode his horse up onto the sidewalk with the intention of riding right into the store. But the doorway was not high enough and he dismounted, leaving the horse in front of the door.

That was the moment Wes Tancred stepped out of the Bon Ton Café, across the street from Fugger's Store. He saw Harpending, gun in hand, plunge into Fugger's place.

Tancred started swiftly across the street. One of Harpending's friends sent his horse forward to cut off Tancred.

"Where do you think you're going?" he demanded.

"Into the store, where else?"

The cowboy noted the lack of armament on Tancred. His code forbade him to shoot an unarmed man and while he hesitated as to how to stop Tancred, the latter went past him into the store.

Inside Fugger's Store, Harpending was advancing toward the rear. On the right, Laura Vesser watched his progress with trepidation. Two other clerks, one a middle-aged woman, the other an elderly man, were backing away before Harpending.

"I want to see the old coot," Harpending was saying. "He told the marshal to arrest me and I wanna know why."

Bill Bleek came down the stairs from the perch in the rear of the store.

"Get out of here, Harpending, if you know what's good for you."

"Well, if it ain't Mr. Fugger's errand boy," sneered Harpending. "And without a gun as usual."

"I don't fight with guns," Bleek retorted, "but if you'll put down your own gun, I'll break every bone in your body."

Harpending raised his rifle, took a careless shot at Bill Bleek. The bullet missed by inches but stopped Bleek on the stairs.

Laura Vesser could not repress a little scream and thus called Harpending's attention to her.

"Hey, what's this? Purtiest girl I've seen in Kansas." He swerved and headed toward Laura Vesser.

At that moment Tancred entered the store. Harpending did not see him. He continued toward Laura.

"I'm a ring-tailed civet cat," declared Harpending, "if you ain't got all the girls down at Ma Hanson's beat a mile. Here—gimme a kiss."

He had reached the counter and suddenly lunged across it. Laura dodged and started away behind the counter.

Harpending wheeled to follow and walked into the swiftly advancing Tancred. Harpending yelped in surprise, tried to lever a fresh cartridge into the chamber of the rifle, but Tancred grabbed it savagely out of his hands and threw it to the floor. Harpending went for his revolver, but it never cleared the holster.

Tancred's fist smashed into Harpending's face. He crossed with a savage blow into the midriff and as Harpending gasped and folded forward Tancred hit him the third and last time, a stunning blow on the jaw. Harpending collapsed.

Tancred stooped and grabbing Harpending by the belt yanked him up. Bleek came forward.

"If you ain't the goddamdest hero!" he snarled.

Tancred shot him a look of complete contempt and propelled the half-conscious Harpending to the door. He whipped it open with his left hand, then braced up Harpending with both hands.

"Here's your friend," he said to the Texas men outside the door.

He shoved Harpending violently forward. The Texas man caromed off one of the horses, hit the hitchrail and fell on his face in the dirt of the street.

The three friends of Harpending stared at Tancred in amazement. Harpending was their leader. His downfall filled them with consternation. One of them half pulled a gun on Tancred, but lacking Harpending's lead he let the gun slide back.

Tancred did not even look back. He went stiffly down the sidewalk, past the hotel. Chuck Gorey, having peered out of the saloon and seeing that Harpending had moved away, was coming cautiously out of the saloon. He stared at Tancred in amazement.

"Is that Harpending back there?" he asked.

Tancred shook his head carelessly, went past Gorey. Jacob Fugger popped out of the saloon and looked after Tancred.

Tancred continued on to the corner, turned and entered the print shop.

"What's all the shooting?" Luke Miller asked.

"Just the usual," Tancred replied. "Drunken Texas men."

But it wasn't more than then minutes before Miller

had the complete story from a visitor. Miller wrote it all down and made certain to give the copy to Mose Hudkins to set up. In the meantime, Tancred was setting up the type for Miller's editorial.

Chapter 10

The last copy of the *Star* was taken away from the press by Mrs. Miller, shortly after four o'clock. The publisher's wife was a plump woman of forty-five, who always criticized what her husband did and always stood behind him on his decisions.

A couple of boys who came in on press day were counting out bundles to deliver to stores and various places around Sage City where the *Star* was sold.

Miller picked up a damp newspaper and let his eyes skim over the front page. An ironical smile twisted his lips.

"And now, the explosion."

"I've read it," said Mrs. Miller. "You just can't take things easy, can you?"

"When a thing's got to be said, it's got to be said," replied Miller.

"But do you have to be doing the saying all the time?"

Miller shrugged easily. "I'm a newspaper man." He turned to Tancred. "What do you think of the Harpending story?"

"You wrote it."

"You wish I hadn't?"

"It was news, I guess, so it had to be printed."

Miller sobered. "I'd write it if it was about myself. If you print the news about other people you've got to print it about yourself," Miller said. "Well, the paper's out, so we might as well call it a day."

Mrs. Miller came over to Tancred. "If it wasn't press day I'd ask you over to supper, but on Thursdays we only have leftovers."

"That's quite all right, ma'am," Tancred said.

The Millers left the shop with the delivery boys who were also taking a bag of mail copies to the post office.

Mose Hudkins puttered about a few minutes, then went

home and Tancred was left alone in the shop. The cot on which he was to sleep was set up in the rear of the shop, but it was scarcely four-thirty.

He washed himself, then took a turn or two around the shop. Finally he left the shop and walked to the Texas Saloon.

Lily Leeds was either in her office or out of the saloon, but two of the bartenders were reading the *Sage City Star*. One of them came over to wait on Tancred.

"Man, oh man, I'd like to see old Jacob's face."

Bill Bleek climbed the steps to Fugger's office on the balcony of the store. He laid the paper on his employer's desk, then stepped back.

Fugger read the editorial in cold silence. When he finished he cursed once, bitterly. Then he read the rest of the paper, skimming through the social and personal items. Finally he swung his chair around.

"He's gone too far," he said to Bill Bleek.

Bleek nodded. "Well?"

"It's too late to talk to him. He's got to have a lesson taught him."

"Some broken bones?"

Fugger hesitated, frowning. "A lot of people like him." He shook his head. "No, don't hit him. Just a warning."

Bleek nodded. He walked down the stairs and out of the store to the office of the *Sage City Star*. He peered through the window and saw that the place was empty. He grinned wickedly and opened the door.

He went past Luke Miller's desk in front and stepped up to the printing press. He knew nothing of printing but even to his unpracticed eye this was obviously the machine that printed the paper.

It was too big, too heavy for one man to turn over without leverage, so he searched until he found a hammer and light-heartedly broke a few rods and bars that were not too massive and smashed a few teeth out on some gears and cogs.

He spied the typecases and pulled out the drawers, dumping the type in a heap, then kicking it about the shop. He knocked over a stock of newsprint, found some cans of ink and dumped them onto the newsprint. He knocked over the paper cutter and broke a bar on it.

That was all the real damage it seemed that he could

do, but on leaving he saw Miller's desk and with a heave sent it crashing loudly to the floor on its side.

He left the shop, pleased with his work. He regretted that Tancred had not been in the print shop.

The courtroom was a rectangular room over the marshal's office and the jail. It contained a half dozen chairs, some benches and a plain wooden table with an armchair at one end. Hong Kong Smith and a half dozen Texas men were in the courtroom when Chuck Gorey brought Harpending up the stairs into the room. Harpending was only half sober and quite unchastened.

Judge Olsen banged his wooden mallet on the table. "Bring the prisoner before the bar," he said officiously.

Gorey nudged Harpending and the Texas man, having seen his friends, whirled and snarled at the deputy marshal. "Don't shove me around!"

Gorey looked gloomily past the prisoner toward Hong Kong Smith. "The judge wants you up front," he said, with restraint.

Harpending swaggered up to the judge's table. "It was self-defense," he growled. "I caught him cheatin' and he pulled his gun on me."

"Just a moment, Mr. Harpending," Judge Olsen said. "This has got to be done legal-like and according to Blackstone. You got to be sworn in, to tell the whole truth and nothin' but the truth, so help you God? Do you?"

"Do I what?"

"Do you swear to tell the truth?"

"You callin' me a liar?" Harpending asked belligerently.

"No—no," replied the judge hastily. "But you've got to be sworn in. That's customary." The judge's worried eyes saw Jacob Fugger and Bill Bleek entering the courtroom and he brightened. "See here, prisoner, you'll do what you're told or I'll fine you for contempt of court."

Hong Kong Smith pushed forward. "Now, wait a minute, Judge. This man works for me and I'm going to see that he gets a square deal . . ."

"He'll get it," snapped Fugger, coming forward.

"He'd better," growled Smith.

Fugger signalled to the judge. "Proceed with the trial, Your Honor."

"That's what I'm trying to do." The judge fixed his

shifty eyes once more on the prisoner. "Now, do you swear to tell the truth, the whole truth and nothing but the truth, so help you God . . . ?"

"I just told you . . ." Harpending began to bluster again, but Hong Kong Smith dropped his huge hand on his shoulder.

"Do as he says."

"All right, I swear."

"Good," said the judge. "Now, let's see, You're charged with shooting one Henry Thatcher, said Henry Thatcher being now deceased. How do you plead, guilty or not guilty?"

"Not guilty," said Hong Kong Smith, calmly. "I saw the whole thing. The dealer pulled his gun on Harpending and Harpending shot in self-defense."

The judge sent a quick look at Fugger. The latter nodded. The judge exhaled in relief. "Were there any other witnesses?"

Hong Kong Smith signalled to his crowd. "These boys all saw it. Did't you, boys?"

The Texas men gave their answers in a single chorus. "We sure did!"

Judge Olsen nodded amiably. "In that case, I find the prisoner not guilty."

The Texas men, including Harpending, let out a whoop of approval. It took Judge Olsen a full thirty seconds of pounding with his mallet to bring them to silence.

"There's another charge against Mr. Harpending," he announced. "Disturbing the peace. I find the prisoner guilty as charged and fine him twenty-five dollars."

Hong Kong Smith scowled. "Now, wait a minute. . . ."

But the little judge pounded the table with his wooden hammer. "The prisoner will pay the twenty-five dollars, plus six dollars costs or go to jail."

Fugger signalled to Hong Kong Smith. The big Texas man hesitated, then reached into his pocket and brought out a fistful of money. "Here's your money, Judge, but I don't mind telling you that I don't like it."

Fugger stepped up beside Smith. "We can't turn him altogether free, Hong Kong. Not after what Miller printed in his paper today."

"The hell with Miller and his paper," snorted Hong Kong Smith. "I bring my herds to this town and I spend a lot of money here. I expect a few small favors in return. If I don't get them, I can take my business to Dodge . . ."

"Where Wyatt Earp'll make your boys toe the line," snapped Fugger.

"There're other places."

"Let's talk about it," suggested Fugger. "Dinner's almost ready. Let's go to my house and have dinner and talk things over."

Hong Kong Smith scowled. "You got anything to drink at your place?"

"I don't drink myself," said Fugger, coldly. "But I guess there's a bottle or two in the kitchen. . . ."

"That's more like it." Smith turned, waved to his men. "All right, boys, you can go now. Have fun and I'll see you all later on."

Harpending swaggered over. "Who's the damn Yankee who hit me when I wasn't looking? I got a score to settle with him." He whirled, grabbed Gorey's shirt-front in his fist. "It wasn't you, was it?"

Gorey looked steadily at Jacob Fugger. The latter shrugged.

Gorey said, "His name is John Bailey. You'll find him at Luke Miller's newspaper shop."

Harpending and his followers streamed out of the courtroom. Gorey turned to find Lily Leeds standing just inside the door, her eyes on him.

"After this," Lily said to the deputy marshal, "stay out of the Texas Saloon."

"I may have to come in now and then," said Gorey, thinly, "to see that you're running a clean place. I'm the new marshal of Sage City."

Lily turned and found Fugger coming toward her. "Is that true, Mayor Fugger?"

"Somebody's got to be marshal," Fugger replied, testily. "Kinnaird quit, so I appointed Gorey to take his place."

"Then Heaven help Sage City!"

Tancred was on his second beer when Lily Leeds came in from the street. She was about to go into her office when she saw Tancred.

"Come in," she said. "Bring your beer with you."

Tancred carried the glass into her office. It was a tiny room, furnished simply with a rolltop desk, two chairs, a couch and an iron safe. There was a closet at the rear where Lily kept several changes of clothes.

"I just came from the courthouse," Lily said. "Judge Olsen tried Manny Harpending."

"And?"

"He killed McCoy's faro dealer in self-defense. A clear-cut case, with a half dozen witnesses who saw the dealer draw first . . . the witnesses being Mr. Hong Kong Smith of Texas and various other Texas men who work for Mr. Smith. But don't worry, justice triumphed. Mr. Harpending was tried on another charge, disturbing the peace, and he was found guilty." She paused. "He was fined twenty-five dollars and Mr. Smith paid the fine. Now . . . about you. The train doesn't leave until morning, but I don't think you ought to wait that long."

"I'm not going anywhere."

"You missed what I was trying to tell you. Harpending's free. He's a Texas man and all Texas men are proud. You humiliated him and he's got to wipe that out."

"He can't taunt me into a gunfight."

"Are you so sure of that?"

Tancred hesitated only briefly. "Yes."

"I hope so, John, I hope so." Then she blinked. "Hey, wait a minute, this is Lily Leeds." She looked at Tancred, her eyes wide. "Well, whaddya know, I was worrying about you."

"Don't, Lily."

A faint smile flitted over her lips. "I haven't worried about anyone but myself in a long while. I'm twenty-four years old. When I'm twenty-eight, Lily Leeds will disappear. And somewhere, maybe in Chicago, New York or even Paris, a widow will appear. A young widow of quality. She will have inherited a considerable fortune from her deceased husband and she will marry even greater wealth." She stopped a moment. "Just four more years."

Tancred nodded thoughtfully. "You'll make it, Lily."

"I know I will. Nothing matters, but that. It's the only thing in this world that matters." She paused again. "And you, John?"

He shrugged.

Lily shook her head. "You're a marked man. Violence breeds around you. Oh, I know, you think you can avoid it. Like now. You humiliated one of the worst men ever to come out of Texas and you think you can avoid fighting him . . . to the finish. And what was it at Turkey Crossing? What was the provocation there?"

"They killed a man who didn't have a chance."

"But wasn't there a girl there? The daughter of the station agent?"

"Yes."

"Yet you rode away after killing the outlaws?"

Tancred put down the emptied beer glass. "I guess I'll go and have some supper."

Lily laughed, but there was no humor in it. "I don't blame you. I just can't keep my mouth shut. But you won't stay away, will you? You'll come back?"

Tancred nodded and went out.

He had a supper of boiled potatoes, steak, apple pie and coffee and when he finished it was after six o'clock. He walked back to the *Star* office, his mind preoccupied and he was inside before he became aware of Bill Bleek's vandalism.

A groan was torn from his throat. He walked through the shop. The type was undamaged, but it would take all of them a dozen hours to sort it out so it could be used again. The press could be repaired, but new parts would have to be obtained and no printing press parts were available closer than St. Louis.

A cold rage seeped through Tancred. A physical injury to a person he could understand, but to destroy machinery and dump out type like this that would consume maddening hours of painstaking toil. . . .

Lee Kinnaird, standing across the street from the newspaper office, watched Tancred go into the shop. He waited a moment, then started across the street. He was halfway across when a pair of mounted Texas man swirled around the corner from South Street and bore down upon the print shop. One of the riders was Manny Harpending.

Kinnaird stopped in the middle of the street and the Texas men pulled up their horses.

"Where do you think you're going, Manny?" Kinnaird asked quietly.

"You ain't the marshal of this town any more," sneered Harpending.

"That's right, I'm not," said Kinnaird, calmly. "I quit this afternoon, because Jacob Fugger wouldn't let me kill you."

"I ain't afraid of you, Kinnaird," blustered Harpending. "Any time you're looking for a showdown. . . ."

"What's the matter with right now?"

Harpending moistened his lips with his tongue. He knew Kinnaird's reputation. A man had to be awfully good and very sober to draw a gun against him.

"I got no quarrel with you," Harpending growled.

"Then turn your horse and ride out of town—and stay away."

Harpending hesitated. The Texas man with him regarded him in astonishment. "You gonna let him get away with that?"

"This is Lee Kinnaird," snarled Harpending. "You fight him if you want to." He whirled his horse and sent it galloping away. His friend was close behind him.

Kinnaird relaxed. He glanced toward the print shop, then turned and walked back across the street.

Inside the print shop, Tancred stared down at the bundle in his carpetbag. A long slow sigh escaped his lips, then he closed the carpetbag and put it under the cot. He sent one more glance about the shop, then left and walked to South Street.

Fugger's Store was closed for the day. Tancred tried the door, then stepped to the street and picked up a rock as big as his fist. He heaved it through the glass of the door, then reached inside the aperture and shot back the bolt. He went inside and started automatically for the right, then swerved and went over to the left side. He put his foot against the grocery counter, gave a shove and knocked it over on its side. Stepping on it, he reached to the top of the shelving, gripped it firmly and backed away.

The shelves came over and merchandise spilled over the floor. Tancred got some bolts of cloth and dumped them onto the groceries, then performed the *coup d'éclat. He* found a barrel of blackstrap molasses and kicked it over so that molasses poured over the groceries as well as the bolts of gingham and muslin.

Most of Tancred's anger went with that but there was still a little left so he climbed the stairs to Jacob Fugger's office and emptied all the drawers of Fugger's desk onto the floor and kicked the papers around a little.

He was quite cheerful by that time and descended to the

main part of the store. Four or five people were standing just outside the door as he came out.

"Tell Jacob it was John Bailey," he told them, "and I'll be at McCoy's Saloon for twenty minutes."

Chapter 11

It was fifteen minutes later when Bill Bleek came into McCoy's Saloon. He found Tancred at the bar with an untouched glass of beer in his hand. A happy expression was on the big man's face.

"I'm glad you paid back the visit, Bailey," Bleek purred. "It wouldn't have been half the fun if you hadn't."

"How are you going to fight?" Tancred asked.

"The way I always fight. For keeps."

Bleek peeled off his coat and tossed it on the bar. A bartender called for McCoy and the saloon-keeper rushed up from the rear. He sized up the situation instantly.

"Not in here, Bill!" he cried out.

"Jacob will pay for the damage," Bleek said. To Tancred, "Oh, he's really mad. The molasses, you know."

"That was for the ink," Tancred said.

Bleek nodded. "Oh, sure." He stepped toward Tancred, grinning.

Tancred smashed the heavy beer glass into Bleek's face. He followed instantly with his left into Bleek's stomach and was appalled by the muscular hardness of it. Yet Bleek reeled back. He wiped beer and blood from his face.

"All right, Bailey," he said. "But don't ask me to quit."

He sprang forward and threw his right fist at Tancred's head. Tancred rolled aside, lashed back. His fist connected but his body also encountered Bleek's left, a solid ramrod of sinew and bone.

Tancred staggered back and Bleek crowded forward. His right connected with Tancred's head, his left flailed into Tancred's stomach. A roaring filled Tancred's head and then Bleek's right exploded again on his jaw and the floor rushed up to Tancred. He fell to his knees and threw out both hands to brace himself against a complete

57

collapse. He remained there an instant—until Bleek kicked him savagely.

Bleek had meant it. It was to be a fight to the finish. Total unconsciousness would not stop it. Bleek would still kick in his ribs and batter his head.

Tancred dropped flat upon the floor, called on his reserves and rolled aside. Bleek's hobnailed boot grazed the skin of his face and Tancred grabbed the foot and twisted hard. Bleek crashed to the floor.

He landed hard and for a moment the breath was knocked from him. He made his feet to find that Tancred was up and grabbing at a nearby chair. Bleek lunged forward. Tancred smashed the chair over Bleek's head. It shattered to splinters and Bleek dropped to his knees.

Tancred lurched forward, caught the bar's edge to keep from falling and saw before him a bungstarter. He grabbed it up, whirled and faced Bleek coming up. He hit Bleek twice with the bungstarter and then it broke.

Bleek's face was streaming blood. His scalp was matted with blood but he still came at Tancred.

"Stand still," he grated thickly. "Stand still and fight."

Tancred hit him, in the face, in the stomach. He hit him four times and Bleek hit him once and Tancred staggered back. He didn't fall and his back touched the bar. Bleek caught him there. He threw his arms about Tancred and put on pressure.

His fetid breath was foul in Tancred's face but the pain was in Tancred's back, where Bleek's hands, locked, were grinding into his spine.

He belabored the big man's head with blows, chopped at his muscular neck with the edges of his open hands. Bleek's grip grew tighter and Tancred could scarcely breathe. With a tremendous effort he got the heel of his left hand under Bleek's chin and forced it up an inch. He got his right hand under the chin and muscled it up another inch. Then he slipped his left hand down to get a firmer leverage and holding the head up with his left hand alone smashed his right hand into Bleek's already bloodied face.

It was a last ditch effort. There was no breath left in his body, his lungs were threatening to collapse. He hit Bleek's nose, his eyes, his cheeks. Again and again, savagely. A groan came from the other man's lips. Tancred struck once more and Bleek let go. He reeled away, blinded in pain and for a long moment Tancred could not follow.

Air rushed into his tortured lungs. He gasped and heaved. Then Bleek, by sheer instinct, lurched forward once more.

Tancred hit him. Bleek's stomach muscles had lost their rigidity. His fists sunk deep. Groans came from the bruiser. Bleek swayed but did not fall. Tancred smashed his face, over and over. Bleek's hands hung helplessly at his sides. His great body quivered.

Tancred stepped back. His fists weighed a ton each. He could not lift them to hit Bleek again. And Bleek was still on his feet.

Jacob Fugger stepped out of the crowd and took Bleek's arm. He turned him toward the door. And Bleek moved as Fugger led him out.

Tancred looked around a ring of quiet faces. Most of them were Texas men but there was now no hostility in them. There was no friendliness either.

Until Lee Kinnaird's face appeared. He stepped up to Tancred.

"Where do you want to go?"

"Miller's shop."

Kinnaird took Tancred's arm and led him out of the saloon. On the sidewalk he saw that Tancred could walk alone and let go of his arm. But he went with him to the print shop and helped Tancred take off his coat and bloodied shirt. He whistled softly as he saw the bruises on Tancred's body.

"You're hurt."

Tancred nodded and dropped heavily to his cot, but only to a sitting position. Kinnaird found a bucket of cold water, a towel. With an effort Tancred raised himself to his feet and soaking the towel in the bucket, sloshed his chest and stomach and arms.

Kinnaird watched and after a while he said, "That's the first fight Bleek ever lost."

"*I* don't feel like I won it."

"You didn't lose, so you won." Kinnaird paused. "He'll be after you again. If he can't beat you with his fists he'll try another way."

"I suppose so."

"And Manny Harpending? You'll have to fight *him* sooner or later."

Tancred dropped the soggy towel into the bucket of
water. He exhaled wearily. "I've been thinking it was
a mistake coming to Sage City."

"That's what I said, when I first came here."

"But you're leaving now."

Kinnaird hesitated, then shook his head. "That's what
Fugger would like me to do, now that I've given him back
his badge. But I've saved a little money and I think I'll
stick around a spell."

The front door of the shop burst open and Luke Miller
charged in.

"John! You're all right?"

"I'm all right," Tancred said, "but the shop isn't." He
gestured about the litter on the floor.

Luke Miller groaned. "It'll take us a week to sort out
the type."

Mrs. Miller came hurrying into the shop. Tancred expected her to bemoan the damage, but she scarcely looked
at it. Her eyes were on Tancred.

"I heard what you did to Jacob's place," she said. "A
barrel of molasses!"

"That was for the ink," said Tancred, pointing.

"I think we got a little the better of it." She reached
for a printer's apron. "Well, let's get busy!"

Luke Miller chuckled. "That's a woman for you. She
complains of every little thing that happens around here,
then something serious comes along and she says, 'Let's
get busy'!"

Chapter *12*

The next morning Luke Miller boarded the eastbound train for St. Louis.

"I only hope they have the parts in St. Louis," he said before he left. "If they have I'll be back in three days, but if I have to go on to Cincinnati. . . ."

"Then we'll miss an issue," said Mrs. Miller.

"It'll be the first time." Miller frowned. "And the last."

He went off and Mrs. Miller, Tancred and old Mose resumed their monotonous sorting of the type. They worked steadily until noon and made scarcely an impression on the heap. Tancred ached in every muscle but oddly enough had greater mental peace than he had had in a long time.

What the talk was in town he did not know. There were two or three callers at the shop but Mrs. Miller went forward and talked to them in low tones. Shortly before noon she left and returned with a basket containing sandwiches and coffee.

After the lunch they worked straight through until six when Mrs. Miller called a halt. "I can't tell a 'b' from a 'p' any more," she declared. "There's only so much of this you can do at a time."

"We're more than half through," said Tancred. "We'll finish tomorrow."

Mrs. Miller and Mose went off. Tancred washed up and walked to the Bon Ton Café. He had scarcely entered when Bill Bleek came in.

His face was puffed and bruised, both eyes were blackened and the left closed entirely. He said to Tancred, "I can still lick you."

"I won't fight you again," Tancred declared. "Not with my fists."

Bleek made an impatient gesture. "Jacob wants to see you."

"I don't believe he can tell me anything I'd be interested in hearing."

"It's for your own good."

Tancred shook his head. "No."

"Jacob Fugger owns this town," Bleek went on. "Luke Miller don't think so but he'll find out.. . . . I'll tell Jacob you'll be over."

"He'll have a long wait."

Bleek peered at Tancred from the one eye that retained vision. "Don't get Jacob mad at you."

He went out.

Tancred ate his supper and paid for it. As he left the café Jacob Fugger called to him from across the street. "You, Bailey, come over here."

Tancred looked at Fugger, then turned away deliberately. Fugger yelled after him, but Tancred continued on. Fugger looked after him, then went into the store.

Bleek stood just inside. "Find me Smith," Fugger said.

"He's next door in the Texas Saloon."

"Get him."

Bleek went out and Jacob Fugger turned and surveyed his store. The clerks were putting away merchandise, preparing to close up for the day. Fugger's eyes came to rest upon Laura Vesser. He studied her for a moment, then walked over to her counter.

"You're a very pretty girl," he said bluntly.

Laura regarded her employer in alarm. Until now, for all the attention he had paid her, she might have been a store fixture.

"Don't worry," Fugger went on. "I'm too old a dog to start that stuff. When I was young, I was too poor to get married and now I've got too much money. But I've noticed that there are quite a few men coming into the store since you're here. And they're buying things they haven't got any use for."

"I'm sorry, Mr. Fugger," began Laura. "I've sold them only the things they ask for. . . ."

"Sell them anything. It's none of your business if they can use the merchandise or not." He nodded shrewdly "Lee Kinnaird's been coming in a lot. He's taken up with that whatsisname who works for Luke Miller."

"John Bailey?"

Fugger grunted. "Bailey, yes. I forgot. He stopped that wild Texan from annoying you yesterday."

He pursed up his lips. "On your way home, would you mind stopping at the newspaper office and telling this, whatsisname, Bailey, that I'd like to see him. You go that way, don't you?"

"Why yes, I do, but . . ." Laura hesitated, then suddenly nodded. "Very well."

"Good. You might as well run along now. Leave things as they are."

Laura got her hat and jacket. Fugger waited until she had left the store, then suddenly shouted to his other clerks, "Close up now."

A few minutes later when the clerks had gone, Hong Kong Smith entered. He was almost sober.

"That bruiser of yours said you wanted to see me."

"I guess I had something on my mind, but I've forgotten now what it was."

Hong Kong Smith bared his teeth in a grin. "I don't think you've ever forgotten anything, Jacob. Come on, what new scheme are you plotting?"

"This man of yours, Harpending . . . I haven't seen him around today."

Smith's eyes narrowed. "Neither have I."

"Has he left for Texas?"

"He won't be going back to Texas."

"Why not?"

"He doesn't like Texas any more," Smith chuckled. "Or maybe it's Texas that doesn't like him. If you know what I mean."

"I think I do."

"All right, let's stop beating about the bush, Jacob. What do you want with Harpending?"

"Do I really have to tell you that, Smith? I gave you a run-down last night on the situation here. All right, I'll spell it out for you. I want two or three men for a month or so, until things get squared away."

"Gunfighters, eh? Mmm, Harpending's all right, but I've got a man down in Texas who'd put two bullets into Harpending while Harpending was trying to draw a gun."

Fugger looked steadily at Hong Kong Smith. "Can you get him up here for me?"

"You can buy anything . . . or anyone . . . for money," said Hong Kong Smith.

Tancred was sorting out type when he heard the door open. He looked over his shoulder and exclaimed softly.

Laura Vesser had entered the shop and was coming

toward him. She said stiffly, "I'm here on an errand for my employer. He wants to see you."

"He'd stoop to anything!"

"And you?" she flashed at him. "I saw what you did to the store."

"But you didn't see what Bleek did here." Tancred pointed to the type he was sorting. "It doesn't look like much, but three of us have been sorting all day. And Mr. Miller's gone to St. Louis to get new parts for the press that Bill Bleek broke. If Bleek had known just a little more about machinery he'd have put the *Star* out of business for keeps."

"But why you?" cried Laura Vesser. "Why do you have to fight Fugger and Bleek? Miller's quarrel isn't yours."

"In all this world," Tancred said, soberly, "the thing I hate the most is a fight."

"Then why *do* you fight?" she flashed at him.

He said, "Sometimes a man can't help but fight."

She turned and went halfway to the door. Then she stopped, her head lowered. Finally she turned. "I'm sorry," she said, quietly. "My father's fight at Turkey Crossing wasn't your fight either."

She went out.

Tancred sorted out a few pieces of type, then took off his shop apron and put on his coat. He left the shop and walked to Fugger's store. As he came up to the place, Hong Kong Smith came out.

The big Texan gave him a hearty half-salute. "Good evening, Mr. Bailey."

Tancred nodded and went into the store. "I got your message," he told Jacob Fugger.

"Oh, Bailey," growled Fugger. "How are you?"

Tancred made a small, impatient gesture, to dismiss the trivialities and to indicate that Fugger should get down to the subject.

"They tell me you're a good man, Bailey," Fugger said.

"You didn't send for me just to tell me that."

"In a way I did," replied Fugger. "I like a good man. I like to have him on my side."

"I'm working for Luke Miller."

"How much is he paying you?"

"Enough."

"I doubt that. He can't afford it. He's got a hundred and eighty-two dollars in the bank and he still owes over six hundred dollars on his print shop equipment. His gross income last month was three hundred and fourteen dollars and fifty-five cents."

"You seem to know quite a lot of Mr. Miller's affairs."

"I make it my business to know everything. If Miller's paying you twenty-five dollars a week, he's drawing down about ten dollars a week for himself."

"He's paying me only twenty dollars a week."

Jacob Fugger snorted. "For a man of your caliber?"

"Mose Hudkins can set up more type than I can."

"A typesetter!" Fugger brushed it away. "Who's talking about setting up type? I saw you beat Bill Bleek with your fists. No man has ever done that before. And they tell me you're a fancy man with a revolver, and that's something Bleek's no good with. I can use a man with your qualifications."

"To kill Luke Miller?"

Jacob Fugger actually chuckled. "You like to call a shovel a shovel. Good. So do I. I'm going to smash Luke Miller. I have to put him out of business because he's threatening *my* business. That's the long and the short of it, I've got to get rid of Miller. I'll kill him if I have to, but I'd rather not. I just want him to close up his newspaper. I want you to work for me and I'll pay you fifty dollars a week."

"It's not enough."

"I pay Bleek only forty a week. How much do you think you're worth?"

"I imagine you're a man, Mr. Fugger, who believes everyone has a price."

"Yes."

"You're probably right. I suppose I have my price, too. I'll tell you what I'll do. I'll leave Sage City tomorrow morning . . ." Tancred paused, "if *you* will."

Fugger exclaimed angrily. "I'm not a humorous man, Mr. Bailey, I don't like jokes."

"You asked me my price and I told you."

"I made you an offer. I now withdraw that offer. Good night, Mr. Bailey!"

Tancred left the store and returned to the print shop. He donned his apron once more and resumed the monotonous job of sorting out type. He worked until midnight and when Mrs. Miller came into the shop in the morning, at seven o'clock, he was already at it.

"I can see now that it was a mistake letting you sleep here," she declared. "You must have been working most of the night.

"There wasn't much else to do."

"Well, you're not going to work tomorrow. Promise that you won't."

"It won't be necessary," Tancred said. "We'll have this all cleaned up by noon."

"Then you'll rest until Monday."

Rest . . . there was no rest for Wes Tancred.

Chapter 13

Saturday was the noisiest day Tancred had ever known in a small town. The cowboys really whooped it up from early morning, through the day and far into the night. Chuck Gorey, the marshal and his deputy, Slattery, remained in the jail most of the day and the Texas men ruled South Street. A faro dealer was wounded and two others suffered bad beatings. A half dozen windows were broken in various stores and one Texas man killed another in a duel.

Sunday morning was quiet. Tancred was awake before daybreak, but remained in the print shop until almost eight. Then he had breakfast at the Bon Ton Café and stood for a little while outside the restaurant. The street was virtually deserted. A church bell tolled north of the Kansas & Western tracks and Tancred blinked. He had not known there was a church in Sage City.

He realized that he knew very little of what went on north of the tracks and decided to take a walk in that direction. It was like entering another world.

There were no saloons on the north side of town, just a few stores that apparently catered to the residential trade, some of whom had businesses south of the tracks, but lived on the north side.

He passed the church, a small, gray-painted frame building. Soberly dressed men and women wearing fine dresses were going into the building.

He returned to the print shop and an odd restlessness kept him from relaxing. The type was all sorted, the print shop was as clean as he could make it and there was no copy on the hooks that he could set. He read some of the old issues of the *Star*, but could not keep his mind on what he was reading.

About ten-thirty he walked to the Bon Ton Café and

had a cup of coffee. When he came out Lee Kinnaird hailed him from across the street.

"Doing anything special?" Kinnaird asked as he came up.

"As a matter of fact, I'm having a hard time doing nothing."

"Then walk with me down there." He pointed to the south of town and Tancred, whose ears were becoming attuned to almost perpetual gunfire, realized that there was shooting out beyond the limits of Sage City.

"There's always a bunch of people out there on Sundays, doing target shooting," said Kinnaird, "and now with the Texas men here we might see some fancy riding and roping." He chuckled. "They even put on a bullfight for us last fall."

Tancred was not especially eager to associate with the uninhibited Texas men, but there was nothing else to do in town and he liked the company of Lee Kinnaird about as well as that of anyone he had met in Sage City.

They walked past the last house on the street to a stretch of flat prairie-land, where a dozen or more Texas men were showing off their skill with horses and the rawhide riatas they had brought with them from Texas. Off to one side another group of Texans were shooting at targets set up. Among the Texans were a few Northerners. As Kinnaird and Tancred came up, one of the latter, a man wearing a Prince Albert and a brocaded vest, was emptying a six-shooter at a board target, fully a hundred feet away. He hit the board each time.

Some of the Texas men were impressed, although one of them stepped up and calmly duplicated the Northerner's feat. The man in the Prince Albert smiled thinly.

"Put the target back a piece," he said.

A cowboy sprang for his horse standing nearby and galloped it to the target. Swinging down low on the right side of his horse he grabbed up the board and carried it back another hundred feet or so. Then he stopped his horse and waved the board.

"Far enough?" he yelled.

The man in the Prince Albert gestured the horseman back. "More!" he called.

The eyes of the entire group were upon him. The horseman rode back further, stopped and looked back. The Northerner pretended not to see him. The horseman accordingly galloped away some more and finally stopped, at a distance of more than three hundred yards from the firing line.

He cupped his hands over his mouth. "This far enough?"

The tall man in the Prince Albert nodded. "Try it there!" he called.

A murmur went up.

Kinnaird nudged Tancred. "Watch this, now."

The Texas men clamored around the tall man in the Prince Albert. "Nobody can hit a target that size with a revolver," shouted one of them.

"They probably can't—down in Texas," retorted the tall man.

"Any Texan can beat any Yank at anything!" howled an irate cowboy.

The tall man pointed at the speaker. "Five dollars says *you* can't hit that target."

"Five dollars says I can if you can," promptly retorted the cowboy.

"That's a bet!"

"And now," Kinnaird whispered to Tancred, "you'll have a chance to see Mr. Wild Bill Hickok . . ."

"Hickok!" exclaimed Tancred.

"The one and only. I heard he got in town yesterday, but I didn't know he was staying over. Guess he needs the money. They don't know they're up against Wild Bill. Watch . . .!"

Wild Bill suddenly thrust out a long-barreled revolver and without seeming to aim, fired. The cowboy on his horse, who had pulled over to one side, galloped up to the target and leaned down from his mount to look at the target. Not believing his eyes he dismounted and examined the target closely. Then he waved.

"He hit it!"

A shout went up among the Texas men surrounding Wild Bill Hickok. The man who had made the bet with him drew his gun. "I still got a chance," he said.

Manny Harpending rode to the firing line from the left where he had been putting his horse through its paces.

"You're a fool, Hodge," he exclaimed. "That's Wild Bill Hickok!"

All eyes went to Wild Bill Hickok. The latter bowed slightly.

Harpending jumped to the ground. "All right if I shoot in place of Hodge?" he challenged Hickok.

"Why not?" Hickok asked coolly.

Harpending drew his gun and took careful aim at the distant target. He fired and all around him could see a splinter fly from the board.

Wild Bill Hickok took a five-dollar gold piece from his pocket and handed it to Harpending. "You shoot very well, stranger."

"Good enough," said Harpending. He tossed the coin to his fellow Texan, Hodge.

"Care to move the target back another hundred yards?" asked Hickok.

"I can hit any target you can hit," snapped Harpending. But he did not look happy about it.

The target was moved back another hundred yards or so and a couple more Texans rode out to watch from the sides. Wild Bill Hickok smiled challengingly at Harpending.

"A small wager?"

"Now it comes," said Lee Kinnaird to Tancred. "I saw him do this in Abilene six years ago. Only then he fired almost six hundred yards. The target was a little larger, but I doubt if there's another man in the entire west who can hit any target at all at six hundred yards."

"Wasn't there a man named Bartles who shot rings around Hickok in a match during the war?" Tancred asked.

"I never heard of it." Kinnaird looked sharply at Tancred. "You're pretty well posted on shooters."

Tancred made no reply. The Texas men had crowded around Will Bill Hickok, making wagers with him. He covered more than a hundred dollars in bets.

He squared off, scarcely took more aim that he had previously and fired. Down near the target the Texas cowboys rode up. A shout went up.

"He hit it!"

A groan went up among the men surrounding Hickok, but Harpending, scowling, took up his position. He aimed and fired. The bullet kicked up dirt a hundred feet short of the target.

"Try it again," said Hickok.

Harpending emptied his revolver at the target, but failed to make a hit.

"Sorry, boys," said Hickok as he collected the bets. He jingled the coins in his hand. "I'll give you all a chance to get it back. Fifty dollars to any man who can hit the target."

"This is what I've been waiting for," said Kinnaird. He nudged Tancred and stepped up to Hickok. "I'll try fifty dollars of that, Mr. Hickok."

The smile faded from Wild Bill's face. "Uh, hello, Kinnaird, didn't see you."

"Shake hands with a friend of mine," said Kinnaird, easily. "John Bailey, Bill Hickok."

Hickok shook hands with Tancred. "Bailey, mm, the name's familiar."

"Mr. Bailey works on the Sage City newspaper. Let's see, the offer was fifty dollars to anyone who can hit the target, eh?"

"A fifty dollar bet," corrected Wild Bill. "Naturally, I'm not just *giving* money away. You've got to risk something, too."

"That wasn't the way I understood it," said Kinnaird. He hesitated, then noting the eyes of the Texas men on him, he nodded. "It's a bet."

He drew his revolver, took careful aim at the target and fired. The scorers examined the target carefully, then waved arms to indicate a miss.

Kinnaird counted out the money, as Wild Bill smiled thinly. "Care to try again?"

"There's a bit of a breeze," said Kinnaird, "makes it hard to figure at the range."

"Let's see Bailey try it," suddenly jeered Manny Harpending. "He's so good with a gun, let's see what he can do."

Tancred stepped back quickly and shook his head. "I haven't got a gun."

"Use the marshal's," cried Harpending. "Let's see if that Turkey Crossing story was poppycock or not."

"Turkey Crossing!" cried Wild Bill. "Of course. That's how I remember the name. John Bailey, eh?" He shook his head. "The name was a new one to me, when I read about that in the Wichita paper and frankly, I . . ." He suddenly beamed. "I'll lend you *my* gun, Mr. Bailey. It shoots as straight as any gun can shoot."

"I haven't got fifty dollars," Tancred said, simply.

"Forget the fifty dollars," Wild Bill said, earnestly.

"I'm anxious to see you shoot." He tendered his revolver, butt first.

Tancred made no move to take the gun. Harpending moved forward. "Come on, Mr. Bailey, let's see you shoot!"

Several of the cowboys took up the chant. Kinnaird whispered to Tancred, "Maybe you'd better try it, Bailey."

"I've never fired a Frontier Model," protested Tancred.

"You're a Navy gun man, eh? Well, I don't blame you. They've never made a gun like them," stated Kinnaird.

"This is a good gun, Mr. Bailey," Wild Bill Hickok said, gently. "I wouldn't use it myself if it wasn't. The trigger pulls light."

Tancred swore softly under his breath, but still did not accept the revolver. Not until Harpending said with a sneer, "Yellow, Bailey?"

Tancred accepted the revolver from Hickok. He hefted it in his hand, then cocked the weapon and let it dangle loosely at his side.

A hush fell upon the augmented crowd of spectators. Tancred raised the gun, thrust it out ahead of him at arm's length and without aiming, fired.

The scorers rushed their horses to the target and one or two dismounted to examine the target closely. A sudden yelp of astonishment went up that carried back to the firing line.

"That's shooting, Mr. Bailey," said Wild Bill Hickok thoughtfully. "Did you say your name was Bailey?"

"John Bailey."

Tancred glanced at Manny Harpending. The Texan's sneer had gone. In his eyes was a look of doubt . . . and fear.

Tancred handed the gun back to Wild Bill Hickok and walked off. The cowboys moved aside to give him a clear passage. Kinnaird followed Tancred.

"That was the best thing you could have done!" he exulted. "Did you see the look on Harpending's face?"

Tancred nodded.

"I'll tell you, now," Kinnaird said, "he was going to go after you. As a matter of fact, I stopped him the other night."

Behind them a man came running.

"Mr. Bailey!" he called.

Tancred looked over his shoulder. The man was Packard, who owned the Boston Store. He stopped and Packard pounded up.

"I saw your shooting, Mr. Bailey," exclaimed Packard.

The former marshal grinned. "You saw mine, too."

"Yes, I did. The range was too far."

"Not for Bailey it wasn't. Or for Wild Bill Hickok."

"I know. If you don't mind, Mr. Kinnaird, I'd like to talk to Mr. Bailey alone."

"Go right ahead." Kinnaird started away, but Tancred detained him with an outstretched hand.

"I don't mind Lee hearing, Mr. Packard."

"I guess it really doesn't matter. Kinnaird's turned in his marshal's badge, which indicates that he isn't on Jacob Fugger's side at least. Anyway, it won't be a secret much longer. The fact is, Mr. Bailey, I've been talking to a few of the people around town and we're getting up a slate of candidates to run against Fugger and his crowd. Luke Miller's down for mayor and—well, we haven't got a name yet for sheriff of the county and I thought, in view of what I've just seen—"

"No," said Tancred, bluntly.

"The office is good for six or seven thousand a year."

"I'm not interested, Mr. Packard," Tancred said, shaking his head. "I'm a printer and that's all I want to be."

Packard was disappointed. "Would you like to think about it a day or two?"

"My mind's made up, right now. I can't think of anything that would make me change it."

Packard let out a slow sigh. "Well, it was a good idea. The marshal, of course, is appointed by the mayor and the city council, but the sheriff's office is an elected one and I'd hoped . . . ." He shrugged. "Thank you, just the same, Mr. Bailey."

He went off and Tancred and Kinnaird walked on into Sage City. Both men were quiet. At the Bon Ton Café they separated and Tancred went on to the *Star* print shop.

Tancred was lying on his cot, looking at the ceiling of the print shop when someone rattled the door-knob. He sat up and peered toward the door, then exclaiming, got to his feet.

Wild Bill Hickok was outside the door.

Tancred unlatched the door and Hickok came in. "I've always been a curious man, Mr. Bailey," he said. "Guns are my business. I've practiced with them since I was kneehigh to a prairie dog. I do a lot of shooting and I've fired against some of the best men in the country. I haven't been beaten by any man in a good many years. But you beat me today."

"It was a lucky shot. And I didn't beat you, Mr. Hickok. Lee Kinnaird said he saw you hit a target once at six hundred yards."

"No man can do that all the time. But since you mention Mr. Kinnaird, didn't I hear you tell him you'd never fired a Frontier Model until today?"

Tancred hesitated, then nodded.

"In other words, you've done your shooting with a Navy Colt." Hickok's eyes became thoughtful slits. "There used to be some fellows over in Missouri, who were awfully good with Navy guns. Ran into them now and then during the war."

Tancred drew a deep breath. "What you're trying to say is that Quantrell's men used the Navy Colt exclusively."

"Yes."

"I rode with Quantrell."

"That's what I figured." Hickok held up his hand. "The war's been over a good many years. I guess everyone knows that I was on the other side, but in recent years I've talked to quite a few of the people who were with you and I've found a lot of them to be pretty decent citizens."

"Thanks," Tancred said, cynically.

"Mmm," mused Hickok. "When I was with Jim Lane in the early days I met a man who was awfully good with a Navy gun. In fact, he outshot me. Ted Bartles. Ran into him a few years ago. Said the boys over in Missouri put up a young chap to shoot against him, back in 'sixty-seven or 'sixty-eight. . . ."

"Donny Pence."

"Ah, you remember!" Hickok chuckled. "Donny was only nineteen or twenty at the time, but Ted tells me he shot rings around him. I guess you'd say that since Ted Bartles beat me and Donny beat him, that would make him just about the best man with a revolver in the country."

"That's possible."

"Bartles said this young Donny never aimed, just threw down his gun like he was pointing it at the target and fired. Wonder what ever became of young Donny."

"I'm not Donny Pence," Tancred said.

"Never said you was. Just talking about shooting. Lot of Quantrell's boys were awfully good with revolvers. Frank and Jesse James, the Younger Boys, Sam Older, Dave Helm." Hickok broke off and studied Tancred a moment.

"Brings back memories, doesn't it?"

"Not pleasant ones."

Hickok sighed. "Don't do to look back, I guess." He shrugged. "I've had my times." He grunted. "You saw what I had to do today to make a few dollars. As a matter of fact, I'm broke. I got married only two months ago and here I am now, away from home, trying to make a stake. I'm on my way to the Black Hills Country. Well, it's been nice talking to you, Mr. Bailey."

He extended his hand, smiling. Tancred shook hands with him.

Hickok started to go, then stopped. He looked quizzically at Tancred.

"There's a name keeps escaping me. There was a boy who rode with Donny Pence and the others during the war . . . some of the boys say he was a better shot even than Donny . . . you wouldn't remember who that was, would you?"

"No," said Tancred.

Hickok nodded. "It's not important. Good-bye, Mr. Bailey."

He went out, on to Deadwood, in Dakota Territory, where he would meet an obscure man named Jack Mc-Call.

Chapter 14

Luke Miller was not on the Monday morning train. Mrs. Miller came into the shop, after going to meet the train, a worried look on her face.

"Apparently he had to go on to Cincinnati. That means he can't possibly return before Thursday morning."

"It wouldn't take more than four or five hours to put the parts into the press," Mose Hudkins said. "If we had the pages all made ready we could still get the paper out by Thursday evening."

"But we haven't got a stick of type set up!" exclaimed Mrs. Miller. "I can write up the local news,' just as I always have, but we need more than that."

"I think I know what Mr. Miller would print on the front page," Tancred said. "The slate of candidates Mr. Packard and some other men are putting up against Jacob Fugger and his crowd."

Mrs. Miller winced. "That's going to mean more trouble."

"Especially since Mr. Miller's name heads the slate."

"No!" cried Mrs. Miller.

"He's the natural candidate for mayor," Tancred went on. "He's led the fight against Jacob Fugger."

For a moment Mrs. Miller looked crushed, but then she drew a deep breath. "I suppose you're right and if Luke were here, I'd back him . . . as usual. Do you suppose you could run over to Mr. Packard's store and get the list?"

Tancred nodded. "I'll go over right now."

He left the shop and walked to the Boston Store. It was a considerably smaller store than Fugger's big place and had only one clerk besides Packard.

Packard brightened when he saw Tancred. "You've changed your mind, Mr. Bailey?"

"No, I haven't. Mrs. Miller sent me over to get the

details about the candidates. Mr. Miller hasn't returned yet and the rest of us are trying to get the paper ready to go to press."

"You *are* going to get out an issue this week?"

"We're going to try."

Packard walked back to his desk and picked up a sheet of paper. He handed it to Tancred. The latter glanced at it.

"Miller for mayor," said Packard, "Fred Kraft for judge, Herb Glassman for prosecutor, besides the six for the council. We still haven't decided on a man for sheriff."

"I'd like to make a suggestion," Tancred said. "Lee Kinnaird."

Packard's eyes narrowed. "Until last week he was a Fugger man."

"He isn't any more."

"You're *sure* of that?"

"As sure as I can be of anything."

"Kinnaird is a very able man, there's no question of that," said Packard thoughtfully. "Except for his former affiliation . . ." He drew a deep breath and exhaled heavily. "Give me an hour. I'll talk to the others."

"I'll start writing this up."

"Good. Oh—I've been thinking. Miller's not going to get a great deal of advertising during the next few weeks so I thought I'd take a rather large ad this week. A half page. . . ."

"I doubt if Mr. Miller would accept a charity ad."

Packard grinned. "The only charity is for myself." He waved about the store. "See any customers? The squeeze is on me as well as on Miller. I've got to go after the people Fugger can't intimidate, the few farmers, the townsmen who can't be hurt by him. The *Star* reaches those people and if I want to stay in business I've got to get them into my store. Here, go see these people." He pointed to the list of names on the slate. "Glassman's a young lawyer who recently hung out his shingle. You're already carrying a professional card from him, but the others are all businessmen around town and all of them are going to be boycotted by Fugger, so they'll need to advertise to get a little business. Call on them."

"I'll do that, but I'll wait until later in the day, after you've had a chance to ask them about Lee Kinnaird."

"I'll let you know on that within the hour."

Tancred returned to the *Star* shop and sat down at a table. He found Mrs. Miller busily scribbling at her husband's desk.

"Did you get the story?" she asked.

"Yes." He hesitated. "You're pretty busy. Would you like me to write it up?"

"I'd appreciate it if you would."

Tancred got a pencil and some paper and went to a table at the rear of the shop. He thought for a moment, then began to write swiftly.

He was still at it when Packard entered the *Star* office. Tancred got up and went forward.

"We've decided to accept Lee Kinnaird," the merchant said.

"I don't think you're making a mistake."

Packard smiled and took a sheet of paper from his pocket. "I brought along the ad I talked to you about and I also talked to the others. They'll all have ads for you."

"Ads!" exclaimed Mrs. Miller. "I hadn't even given that a thought."

"With Fugger laying the boycott on us we've got to advertise to stay in business. At least until the election." Packard paused. "If we lose that, we lose everything."

"We've *got* to win," declared Mrs. Miller.

Packard nodded. He left the shop and Tancred finished writing the story about the forthcoming election. When he finished it, he took it to Mrs. Miller. She scanned it quickly and when she finished she looked at Tancred worriedly.

"Isn't it a—a little strong?"

"I don't know. I tried to write it the way I thought Mr. Miller would write it."

"That's what I meant. It sounds just as if *he* had written it. I—I have a feeling that he would like it very much."

Tancred looked at her inquiringly. She nodded suddenly. "Set it up." Then, as Tancred turned away: "Oh— John, you write very well. How is it you haven't had a newspaper of your own?"

"I'm a printer."

"So is Luke. He was a printer for years before he bought his own paper. And I sometimes wish he was still a printer."

Tancred took the copy back to the type cases and began to set it up. Mose Hudkins was already working on the local news that Mrs. Miller had been writing.

When Tancred went to the Bon Ton Café for his lunch he found South Street even more crowded than it had been the previous week. The second trail herd had reached Sage City that morning and the cowboys were in town, roaming the streets. As yet they hadn't been paid, as they were not Hong Kong Smith's men, but the owner of the herd was expected to reach Sage City the next day and when he arrived and paid his men, the town could expect a repetition of the wild scenes it had seen the past week.

Lee Kinnaird walked down South Street and made a mental list of the enterprises that Jacob Fugger owned or controlled. There was of course the Fugger Mercantile Company, where Jacob made his headquarters. The Sage City Livery Stables and Corral were owned outright by Jacob as was the hay and feed business and the lumber-yard down by the K & W tracks. The Fugger Produce Company which dealt in buffalo and cattle hides and shipped a hundred carloads of buffalo bones every season was another fully owned Fugger business.

Joe Handy was the nominal owner of the Sage City Hotel, but it was pretty generally known in town that Fugger had a large mortgage on the place and could fore-close at any time the fancy struck him. It was not general-ly known that Fugger controlled McCoy's Saloon, but the bank held a note of McCoy's. And the bank, of course, was Jacob Fugger. Horace Van Meter was the cashier, but he owned less than one-tenth of the stock. Fugger owned fifty-five percent and Van Meter never made a loan without first getting Fugger's permission.

Morgan Holt apparently owned his hardware store, but he was under some sort of financial obligation to Fugger so it could be rightly said that Fugger had control of that business too.

The largest single source of revenue to Jacob wasn't really a business at all; it was a simple agreement he had made with the Kansas & Western Railroad back in '71 when Sage City had sprung up from the prairie. The rail-road paid Fugger one dollar for every steer that was shipped from Sage City. With the exception of the first year, when Jacob had spent a certain amount of money to put up the loading pens which were attached to the

railroad siding, all of this revenue was clear profit. Fugger
bought no cattle and he sold no cattle. Buyers from the
Kansas City and Chicago stockyards came to Sage City
in the spring and usually remained in the town until fall.
They dealt directly with the Texas cattlemen. They
bought the steers and paid the cattlemen . . . and Jacob
Fugger received one dollar for every steer that was
counted through his loading pens. In 1875 the railroad had
paid Fugger for one hundred and seventy-two thousand
steers and Fugger estimated that the number would
reach the two hundred thousand mark in the current year.

The K & W paid Fugger a great deal of money every
year, but it had a realistic attitude about it. It would
probably receive much of the freight without Fugger's
assistance, but it would lose much of it, too. The eastern
Kansas towns that had once shipped a considerable number of steers gave the railroad virtually no such freight today. The western towns were closer to the origin of the
beef trade. They cut down the traveling time of the trail
herds by days. But there was competition for the herds.
The Santa Fe reached Dodge City, a wide-open town,
much liked by Texas men. The Santa Fe catered to the
cattle trade.

Certain smart drovers even drove their herds past the
K & W and the Santa Fe and went another three hundred
miles north to the Union Pacific. The grass was good all
the way and by leisurely traveling and grazing of the
herds for a few weeks on the fine grass around Ogallalla
they frequently put meat on the herds that meant extra
dollars to the cattlemen . . . but no revenue to the
K & W.

Fugger diverted many thousands of head of steers from
going to the Union Pacific in the north. He cultivated the
friendship of the Texas cattle drovers and encouraged
many of them to bring herds to Sage City that might
otherwise have gone to Dodge City or other points on the
Santa Fe. The K & W railroad did not mind paying the
dollar a head toll to Fugger of Sage City.

Kinnaird walked down to the railroad depot and saw a
hundred head of restless, bawling steers milling around in
Fugger's loading pens. A cattle train had been shoved
onto the siding and was being loaded for an eastward
trip.

A single box car stood on the west end of the siding.

Seeing some men working in and out of the box car Kinnaird strode over.

Kinnaird recognized two of the men as he came up. They were brothers named Strasser who had settled on the prairie south of town the year before. They were now loading furniture and farming implements into the box car.

"You're pulling out?" Kinnaird asked in surprise.

The older of the Strassers, a squat, heavy-set man of about forty, shrugged. "What else? We put in a hundred acres of wheat in the fall. A week ago it looked like it would run close to fifty bushel to the acre. Today there isn't a blade of it standing."

"Cattle!" snorted the other Strasser brother.

"But your farms were fenced in!"

"*Were* fenced in is right," said the other brother. "Them goddam cowboys broke down the fences. We go to see the marshal and the judge yesterday. The marshal says it's none of his business what happens outside the town limits and the judge says we was only squatters on the land and we had no right to put up fences anyway. All right, we know when we're licked. So do the rest of the farmers who settled here. They'll be pulling out one by one."

"Do either of you happen to read the *Sage City Star?*" Kinnaird asked.

"Sure, we both read it all the time. The editor, Mr. Miller, he was on our side, but he's only one man and—and we heard what happened to his paper last week. They broke up all his machinery and now he's out of business. So are we. We're going back to Illinois."

"You liked it here?"

"Sure, but we got families. We have to live where we can make a living."

"Would you stay in Sage City if, say, Luke Miller were elected mayor, if the county had a sheriff who would keep the cattlemen from breaking down the farmers' fences, and if there was a county judge who protected your rights as well as the rights of other people?"

The younger Strasser guffawed. "You're dreaming, Mister. That'll never happen around here, not in ten years."

"It might happen inside of two weeks," said Lee Kinnaird.

The older Strasser said, "Uh-uh. If Luke Miller was elected mayor of Sage City, Jacob Fugger would have him killed."

Kinnaird turned away from the farmers. Thoughtfully he started back toward the town. As he passed the depot a voice called to him.

"Mr. Kinnaird!"

Laura Vesser was coming out of the depot. Kinnaird brightened.

"Hello," he said, "what're you doing here?"

"Mr. Fugger sent me here with a telegram." She fell in beside him. "Who is Eric Stratemeyer?"

"He's a gambler. At least, that's the way he makes his living, but he's better known for . . ." Then he looked at her sharply. "Why?"

"I just happened to hear his name."

"This telegram that Fugger's sending . . . it was to Stratemeyer?"

Loyalty to her employer caused Laura to become evasive. "I didn't say that. I just wondered about Eric Stratemeyer . . . the name's rather unusual."

"Stratemeyer's an unusual man." Kinnaird nodded thoughtfully. "He's got a reputation for having killed about a dozen men."

Laura shuddered. "You said he was a gambler."

"He's a faro dealer. Most of the men he's killed played against him . . . and all of them drew guns against Stratemeyer. Stratemeyer's never killed a man except in self-defense."

Her forehead became creased as she frowned. "Some men were talking in the store this morning, about Wild Bill Hickok being in town yesterday."

"That's right."

"Is it true that someone beat him shooting?"

"What you want to know," said Kinnaird, "is if John Bailey has a chance against Eric Stratemeyer?"

She gasped. "I didn't say that!"

"You're taking the long way around, but that's what you're getting at, isn't it? Fugger sent a telegram to Stratemeyer and you have reason to believe that he's coming here to kill Bailey."

For a moment she kept her face averted, then she looked at him squarely. There was inquiry in her eyes.

He said, "Your last name is Vesser. You saw John Bailey in action."

She emitted a slow sigh. "I was there when he—when he killed those men, but it all happened so fast that I—I don't know what to think. He's made an enemy of Mr. Fugger and . . ."

"You're worried about him." A note of dullness came into Kinnaird's tone. He hesitated a moment, then shook his head. "I've talked to Bailey. I mean that just the way I said it. I've talked *to* him. But he doesn't answer. I don't know what he's thinking when I talk to him. I don't know anything about him. You knew him at Turkey Crossing."

She laughed shortly, without humor. "I saw him at Turkey Crossing. I saw him every day for six or seven weeks. I never knew him. I guess no one knows him."

Kinnaird nodded. "I saw him shoot against Wild Bill yesterday. He didn't beat him. It wasn't a contest. He hit a target that Wild Bill hit but he fired only once at the target. It may have been a lucky shot. I don't think so, but . . ." He shrugged. "That's John Bailey. He doesn't talk."

Chapter 15

Tancred stood at the bar in the Texas Saloon, a half-emptied glass of beer before him. Lee Kinnaird entered and stood inside the batwing doors, searching the room. He saw Tancred at the far end of the bar, nodded to himself and walked down.

"Evening, John," he said.

"Evening, Lee."

"Gil Packard talked to me this afternoon," Kinnaird said. "He said you suggested my name for sheriff."

Tancred made no reply.

Kinnaird, remembering his talk with Laura Vesser, frowned. "I accepted."

"I hoped you would."

Tancred took a sheet of paper from his pocket, unfolded it and handed it to Kinnaird. It was a proof of the article he had written for the *Star*. Kinnaird read it through carefully, then refolded and handed it back to Tancred.

"That's a pretty strong piece."

"It's intended to be."

"As a matter of fact," Kinnaird said, slowly, "I saw something this morning that kinda made me glad you put up my name for that job. I was down at the depot and talked to a couple of farmers who're pulling up stakes. They tell me that most of the others who've settled here the last year or two intend to leave."

"As long as Fugger runs Sage City there's nothing here for farmers."

"Sage City's all right for Jacob Fugger, but it's no good for anyone else. Yet the country around here is as good land as you'll find anywhere in the state. If we let the farmers come in, Sage City will remain a permanent town."

Lily Leeds came out of her office, looked at Tancred and Kinnaird a moment, then walked over to them.

"Hello," she said, to Kinnaird, then to Tancred. "You came back."

Tancred picked up his glass. "The beer's good."

"And you scared the hell out of Manny Harpending," Lily added, sarcastically, "so you think the Texas men will let you alone."

Kinnaird's eyes showed surprise as he watched Lily Leeds.

"I've no fight with Harpending," Tancred said, shortly.

"That's what you think," retorted Lily. "You humiliated him again yesterday and you think Harpending can let that pass. He's a gunfighter. If you back down a gunfighter he can do one of two things. He can run away . . . or he can kill you. Harpending can't run away. He's got no place to run to."

"He's wanted in Texas," Kinnaird said.

Tancred drank the dregs of his beer. He nodded to Lily and walked off, heading for the door.

Kinnaird's eyes remained on Lily's face. He saw it redden with anger, saw her lips move slightly and barely heard the exclamation under her breath.

"Damn you!"

Kinnaird said, "It's like that, is it?"

For a moment Lily's eyes remained on the door, then Kinnaird's words penetrated and she flashed him a look. "What do you mean?"

Kinnaird shrugged. "Eric Stratemeyer's coming to Sage."

Her eyes remained clouded a moment, then suddenly narrowed. "How do you know?"

"Fugger's sent for him."

She darted another look at the door, through which Tancred had gone.

Tancred stood outside the Texas Saloon. It was a humid night and the thought of going back to the print shop depressed him. And Lily Leeds' scorn—which was not scorn at all—tugged at him. He turned north and walked to the railroad tracks.

He stood for a few minutes on the depot platform, looking at the north side of Sage City. Behind him, on South Street, was the noise of a dozen saloons and honky-tonks, the tinkling of a piano here and there, a voice raised in song, the shouting and whooping of carousing Texas men.

Ahead, was comparative quiet.

Tancred crossed the tracks. The street was dark, lighted only here and there by reflected light coming from a modest home. Tancred was not lonesome; he had lived alone too long for that. He had learned through the years to do with a minimum of talk and contact with people, but tonight a restlessness gripped him.

He walked for a block and crossing a street saw someone coming toward him. Tancred slowed his steps and watched a rectangular patch of light from a house. The person ahead entered the light and he saw that it was Laura Vesser.

She stopped. "Hello."

"The street's not a safe place for a girl at night," he said.

"I walk every night," she replied. "They keep pretty well on the other side of the tracks." She paused. "I haven't seen you here before."

"I haven't done much walking."

"You're living at the newspaper shop?"

"Yes."

She pointed over her shoulder to a house. "I've a room with Mrs. Martin. She works at the store."

"How do you like working in a store?"

She flashed him a smile. "It's the first job I've ever had and I—I like it."

"Fugger treats his employees well?"

Her smile faded. "I know you don't like Mr. Fugger . . . and I've heard other people complain of him. But he's been quite good to me. If it wasn't for . . ." She stopped.

"Yes?"

"He looks at me. Several times every day I—I feel someone's eyes on me and I look up to the balcony and he's standing there looking down at me." She shivered a little. "It makes me nervous."

"I don't think you'd have any trouble getting another job."

"But I like the store. It's just . . . I shouldn't have said anything. Mr. Fugger pays me well and the work isn't hard."

She looked over her shoulder toward the house where

she lived. Tancred's directness always disconcerted her. Now that she thought of it, she realized that every contact with him had not only disconcerted her, but caused her . . . pain.

She said, "It's time for me to go home."

"I'll walk with you."

"It's only a short way."

He nodded and fell in beside her. They walked a few steps in silence, then Tancred asked, "You're going to stay in Sage City?"

"I've no other place to go." She shot a look at him. "Are you going to stay here?"

"I'm not sure."

"You don't stay any place very long, do you?" She was unable to keep the tartness out of her voice and it silenced him. They walked to Mrs. Martin's house, a square box of a house with a picket fence surrounding it.

Laura opened the gate.

"Good night."

"Good night," Tancred said. He waited for her to move on into the yard, but she did not.

"I'm sorry," she said in a low tone.

"There's nothing to be sorry about."

"Yes, there is. I—I know who you are and I've been taking advantage of it."

"It doesn't matter."

She half turned, looked intently into his face. "It does matter. It matters a lot, doesn't it? I can't get it out of my mind. Wherever you go there's always someone who knows . . . oh, they may not know you, but they know about you. The night before last a man came to see Mrs. Martin. They—they're sort of friends and he comes here two or three a nights a week. He plays a guitar and he sings. He sang a song about Sam Older . . . and you. . . ."

"I suppose," Tancred said, wearily.

"You've heard the song? People who don't know who you are sing it when you're around?"

"I heard it the first night I came to Sage City. I've heard it a thousand times."

She shuddered. "How can you stand it?"

"You can get used to anything."

"No, that's not true. There are things you don't get used to. Things that—hurt."

"Good night," Tancred said, dully.

"Wait a minute." He stopped. "I—I think talking might help."

"It won't."

"How do you know it won't? You've never tried it. You've gone through all these years, from town to town, place to place . . ."

"It doesn't matter." Testiness crept into his words. "Believe me, it doesn't matter."

He would have turned away again, but her hand came out and dropped on his arm.

"Why did you do it, Wes? Was it . . . like the song says?"

No!" he exclaimed. "It's a lie. It's a lie that's grown so big that it's become the truth. Sure, I killed Sam Older. I've killed a dozen men, perhaps two dozen. Why not? It was all I knew." His voice became bitter, but the dam had broken and he continued on.

"I had a gun in my hand before I was six years old. We grew up with guns, all of us. In western Missouri, where I lived, they were raiding into Kansas in 'fifty-four and Kansans were raiding into Missouri. My father was killed by a Kansan when I was eight years. I was fourteen when the war started and I joined up with Quantrell when I was sixteen. The war on the border was . . . hell. We robbed and were robbed, we murdered and were murdered. Then, suddenly the war ended. I was eighteen years old in 'sixty-five and the only life I knew was violence and death. All right, some of Quantrell's men settled down. I did myself. I got a job in a print shop in Lexington. But they wouldn't let us alone. The Yanks were in the saddle and they made things miserable for us. Some of the boys—Sam Older for one—became outlaws. They made things even worse for the rest of us."

He paused a moment. "I was arrested twice for being an Older man—months before I actually joined up with him. I was kept in jail for six weeks the second time. It was too much. I joined up with Sam, in late 'sixty-six."

He stopped and exhaled heavily. "Yes, I rode with Sam Older. That part of the song is true. But the rest isn't. Sam was no Robin Hood. He didn't steal from the rich and he didn't give to the poor. He didn't go around help-ing poor widows. He . . . he was one of the worst of Quantrell's men. He killed without compunction. When the hue and cry went up for him he became like a—a mad dog. He turned on his own men. That's when I killed him."

He paused again, his mouth twisting bitterly. "But it was a fair fight—as fair as such things can be. I had the edge on him. Older was a good shot with a revolver. He could draw fast and he practiced all the time, but I—I had the knack for it. I could beat Donny Pence. Dave Helm and Dick Small were there and *they* know . . . they know that Older went for his gun first, that I didn't draw mine until his hand cleared leather. . . . Dave Helm and Dick Small know, but they couldn't talk. And soon it was too late. The legend started and it grew. Like the song."

The torrent of words stopped and Tancred stared at Laura Vesser, appalled. Her eyes were intent on his.

She said, softly, "I'm glad you told me."

His hand reached out, took hers. For an instant he gripped it tightly, then he pushed it away, almost roughly. "Good night." He turned and strode off into the darkness and Laura stood by the gate and watched him until he disappeared.

A smile was on her face as she went into the house.

Chapter 16

Luke Miller returned to Sage City on the Thursday morning train. On the train was a pale, drawn-looking man in his mid-thirties. He wore a gray derby, a gray Prince Albert with a gray silk vest. He also wore a broad belt with a holster that contained a nickel-plated, short-barreled revolver.

This was Eric Stratemeyer, whose reputation was known throughout the west.

Mrs. Luke Miller and Wes Tancred, who were at the depot, did not see Eric Stratemeyer. Their eyes were on Luke Miller whose arms were loaded with parcels and two or three wooden boxes. Miller set the packages down on the platform and kissed his wife.

"We'll have a paper next week," he declared.

"We'll have a paper this week," said Mrs. Miller. "We're ready to go to press as soon as the press is ready."

Miller exclaimed. "But how could you? When I left you had a mess of pied type and that's all."

"Just wait and see." Mrs. Miller smiled at Tancred. "Let's get these parts over to the shop."

Tancred was already gathering up an armful of bundles. Miller caught up the rest and they started for the print shop.

Inside the plant of the *Star* Miller stripped off his coat and rolled up his sleeves. "Let's get to work."

"Maybe you'd better read the proofs of the front page," Tancred suggested.

"No hurry. Just the usual local stuff, isn't it?"

"Not quite," said Mrs. Miller. "John's right—take a look at what we've got set up."

Miller caught up the page proofs. He had barely glanced at it, then he exclaimed.

"Mayor! Me?" He read on and as he read a gleam came into his eyes. "I see what you mean," he said, as he continued reading. Finally he looked up and drew a deep breath.

"Who wrote this?"

Mrs. Miller indicated Tancred. "Is it . . . all right?"

"It's great!" cried Luke Miller.

One of the *Star* delivery boys brought a bundle of newspapers into the Fugger Store and deposited them on the counter where Laura Vesser worked. She glanced at the headline and her interest was caught. She read Tancred's article, the frown on her face growing as she read.

Then the newspaper was whisked out from under her eyes by Bill Bleek.

"For the boss!"

Bleek started off with the paper, but began to read it and stopped. He read the entire article on the forthcoming elections, then looked up toward the balcony. He whistled softly, then shrugging, climbed the stairs.

Fugger had begun to total the results of the business of his various enterprises. He looked glumly at Bleek as the latter appeared with the newspaper.

"So they got out a paper, after all!"

"And it's quite a paper."

Fugger took the paper and began to read. A spot of red appeared on his cheeks, began to grow.

"So Miller wants to be mayor," he finally said.

"They were pretty close-mouthed about it," said Bleek, "but I got a hint of it a couple of days ago."

"Why didn't you tell me?"

"It was just a rumor and I couldn't check it. They offered the sheriff's spot to John Bailey, but he turned it down."

"That's crazy. The job'll be good for at least five or six thousand a year."

"He still turned it down."

"There's something about this Bailey I can't put my finger on," said Fugger. "And Miller, too. He's been twice as bad since Bailey's gone to work for him." He leaned back and the faint appearance of what might have been a smile on someone else broke his features.

"A man named Stratemeyer came to town today. . . ."

"I've seen him," said Bleek shortly. "You . . . sent for him?"

"Nobody knows that."

"Three people today told me that you sent for him."

Fugger made an angry gesture. "Stratemeyer hasn't been in here and he isn't going to be. He's going to deal faro for McCoy."

"And what about those gunfighters Hong Kong Smith's bringing from Texas? What're they going to do?"

"Where'd you hear about them?" snapped Fugger.

"Smith likes to talk when he's sober and when he's drunk he talks twice as much." Bleek paused. "You're going to fill up the town with gunfighters." He looked morosely at his employer. "Used to be *I* took care of all these things."

"You didn't take care of Bailey!"

"I can lick him," said Bleek.

"Can you?" sneered Fugger.

Bleek turned and walked heavily down the stairs to the store and out to the street. Fugger's eyes fell to his work, but for a long while he did not see the figures before him.

Bill Bleek was known to take two or three drinks of an evening, but he spaced them out and no one had ever seen him the worse for the drinks. No one had ever seen him sit in a game of chance in Sage City.

That evening Bill Bleek got drunk at McCoy's Saloon and he gambled. He sat in a poker game and lost fifteen or twenty dollars, then he played faro and won fifty dollars. He drank steadily.

And then he finally moved to the faro game of Eric Stratemeyer. Stratemeyer was widely known for his prowess with a gun, but it was also known that he ran an absolutely straight game and his table had a good play.

Bleek played for five or ten minutes and won a few dollars. Then he lost a ten dollar bet and doubled the next bet. He lost that and put out forty dollars.

"I'd better not lose this one," he muttered.

Eric Stratemeyer gave him a sharp look and slid the cards out of his box. "Queen wins, seven loses."

Bleek's money was on the seven. He reached out. "Pay me."

"Seven loses, friend," Stratemeyer said.

Bleek's reaching hand became a fist that darted across the table and exploded on the point of Stratemeyer's jaw. The gambler crashed backwards over his chair, hit the floor with a heavy thud. He scrambled clear and the cheap nickel-plated revolver was somehow in his fist.

The gun roared and a spot appeared in the center of Bill Bleek's forehead. Bleek swayed for an instant, then his body sagged to the floor.

Stratemeyer looked coolly around at the stunned witnesses. "Well?" he asked.

No one said a word.

Lee Kinnaird came into the Texas Saloon and saw Wes Tancred at the bar. He was watching Lily Leeds, who was at the back of the room talking to the piano player.

Kinnaird walked up to Tancred. "Bill Bleek just picked a fight with Eric Stratemeyer." Then, as Tancred looked at him inquiringly, "Bleek found out that a fist's no good against a gun. He's dead."

"Jacob will have a hard time replacing him."

"He's already been replaced," said Kinnaird. "Stratemeyer. Or, didn't you know that Fugger sent for him?"

Tancred shrugged. Kinnaird continued:

"Fugger sent a telegram to Stratemeyer. Laura Vesser told me about it." Tancred's eyes came to Kinnaird's face and the former marshal did not avert his own eyes. "Fugger's deep. It could be he wanted it to leak out that he'd sent for Stratemeyer."

"Possibly," said Tancred.

"You've heard of Stratemeyer's reputation?"

"Who hasn't?"

"I don't suppose it's occurred to you that Stratemeyer's being here has anything to do with . . . you?"

Tancred was spared the answering of that question. Lily Leeds had left the piano and the professor began to play.

An inadvertent tremor ran through Tancred. Then he relaxed and leaned against the bar.

Lily began to sing . . . the saga of Sam Older and the man who had killed him. She sang the song even better than she had sung it the last time Tancred had heard her. She finished to thunderous applause.

"That girl can really sing," Kinnaird said fervently to Tancred.

Tancred nodded.

"She puts a lot of feeling into it," Kinnaird went on. "Especially that song. I've heard her sing it a dozen times and she does it better all the time." Then he added, "Of course, it happens to be one of my favorite ballads."

Lily Leeds came up. "Like it?" she asked Tancred.

"I like your singing."

"Oh yes, that's what you said the last time. But you don't like the song." She smiled at Kinnaird. "But *you* like it!'"

"I've always had a weakness for old Sam Older."

"Sure, he was your kind of man."

"I never met him, but I've talked too two or three people who knew him. They said he was a real curly wolf."

"And to think that a coward like Wes Tancred should kill a man like that!"

"Speaking of killing," said Lee Kinnaird, "Eric Stratemeyer killed Bill Bleek just about ten minutes ago."

She stared at Kinnaird in astonishment. "But . . . but I thought . . ." Her eyes darted to Tancred.

Kinnaird said, thinly, "You thought Fugger had sent for Stratemeyer. Don't discount that, yet. I was in McCoy's when it happened. Bleck was drinking—a lot. That's something he's never done before. And he was gambling. I was watching him and it seemed, well, like Bleek was working around to picking a fight with Stratemeyer."

"But why would he do that?"

"No one will ever know." Kinnaird pursed up his lips thoughtfully. "Except maybe Jacob Fugger."

Lily suddenly turned to Tancred. "Lee stopped me from saying it—that Stratemeyer's in town to kill you."

"Stratemeyer's a gunfighter," said Tancred, "and I don't carry a gun."

"Bleek didn't either," retorted Lily. "Maybe—maybe that's the point of the whole thing, a warning to you."

"Bleek wouldn't let himself get killed just to warn me!"

"But Fugger might have had him killed for that reason," suggested Kinnaird. He looked pointedly at Lily. "I forgot—you're on Fugger's side."

"I'm on my own side," cried Lily. "I've told you that before." She turned on Tancred. "I might even vote for Luke Miller. And you," she said to Kinnaird.

"If I'm elected sheriff," said Kinnaird, "I might have to close you up." He grinned lazily.

Chapter 17

Several days before election, Packard appeared before the town council of which he was still a member and demanded that there be at least one voting place north of the K & W tracks, in the "civilized" part of town.

The councilmen looked toward Jacob Fugger who made a negative gesture with his head. The council voted five to one against Packard. The voting was to be held in the only public building in Sage City, the courthouse, which also contained the marshal's office and the jail.

Packard then demanded that the saloons be closed while the voting was in process. He was out-voted again, five to one. He made one last request, that his faction be allowed three representatives at the polls. Fugger thought this over for a moment, then agreed. He did not see how he could do otherwise as the voting had to be public and too many people would take note of the fact if his adherents only were allowed to watch the ballot box.

The same day, Hong Kong Smith's fourth trail herd of the season reached Sage City. It was also his largest, with no less than thirty of his Texas hellions accompanying the herd. The cowboys who had brought up his third herd were still in town. They had just about squandered their salaries, but there was a whisper of free liquor on Election Day and they intended to take full advantage.

Hong Kong Smith rode out to his newly arrived herd, three miles from Sage City.

The cowboys whooped and surrounded him. "I'm sorry, boys," Smith announced. "I didn't expect you until tomorrow and the bank's closed for the day. But come in bright and early tomorrow and you'll have your money . . . and free drinks the rest of the day!"

A roar went up and guns banged. "See you in the morning!" boomed Smith. He mounted his horse and prepared to ride back to Sage City. As he cleared the camp, he discovered that a cowboy was riding after him.

"Mr. Smith," the man called. "I'm Dave Helm."

Smith pulled up his horse. "You got my message?"

"I wouldn't have left Texas if I hadn't," replied Helm. He was a lean, rather handsome man in his mid-thirties, a man who minded his own business as a rule and who was let alone by the wild Texas cowboys.

Smith nodded. "They don't know much about you in Sage City."

"You've got a sheriff here?"

"Not yet. They're voting tomorrow. There's a marshal, man named Gorey."

"I've heard of him."

"You're not afraid of him?"

"Of his gun, no. Of his badge, yes."

"Gorey takes his orders from Jacob Fugger—"

"—who owns Sage City!"

"And who does what *I* tell him to do," Hong Kong Smith said, importantly. "You haven't got a thing to worry about, Helm. Not a thing."

"I'm taking your word for it, but I've been around a long time. That's because I've always been careful." His eyes narrowed thoughtfully. "This election tomorrow . . . any chance of it going against Jacob Fugger?"

Hong Kong Smith chuckled. He closed one eye in a huge wink.

At seven A.M. Marshal Chuck Gorey hung up a sign outside the marshal's office. On the sign was scrawled, "Vote Here." Gil Packard, Luke Miller and Lee Kinnaird came across the street.

"Gonna vote bright and early," Gorey remarked.

"That's right," said Miller calmly.

They followed the marshal into his office. A wooden box stood on Gorey's desk. Beside it was a stack of ballots. "Help yourself," said Gorey, indicating the box and the ballots.

Packard shook his head. "We'll wait until the polls are officially open."

"They're open now," replied Gorey.

"Fugger was to have three men here," said Packard.

"Seems to me I did hear something about that," Gorey said. "I guess they'll be along. But if you want to vote, go ahead, nobody's stopping you."

"We'll wait," said Luke Miller. "If we expect to have others vote properly, we'll do so too."

Gorey's eyes narrowed. "You three going to sit here all day?"

"The city council voted to have three representatives of each slate of candidates preside over the voting."

"And you fellows picked yourselves?"

"Anything wrong with that?"

Gorey shrugged and left the marshal's office. Five minutes later Jacob Fugger came into the office, alone.

"You fellows don't trust anyone, do you?" he groused.

"You, least of all," snapped Luke Miller.

Fugger bared his teeth in a wolfish grin. "If it isn't the mayor," he sneered.

Miller's eyes flashed and he was about to take up the challenge, but Packard gave him a covert signal and the newspaper publisher turned his back on Fugger.

McCoy, the saloonkeeper, came in. He was followed a few minutes later by Morgan Holt, the hardware man, and Cece Tobin, who ran the feed and produce business in town, one of Fugger's enterprises. Fugger whispered to them a moment or two, then took his departure.

"We're ready when you are," Tobin announced then.

"Good," said Packard. "I suggest we do this with as little argument as possible. As each voter comes in he writes down his name, so we can check on possible repeaters."

"What if he can't write?" asked McCoy.

"If a man can't write he can't vote," snapped Packard.

"Whoa!" cried Morgan Holt. "You can't discriminate against a man just because he can't write his own name. That ain't right. Besides he don't have to write to vote. All he's got to do is put a cross before a candidate's name."

Packard looked inquiringly at Miller. The latter nodded.

"All right," conceded Packard. "We'll write down their names, then."

"Then let's vote," snapped McCoy.

He took up a ballot and made a few quick checks, then folded the ballot and dropped it into the slot of the ballot box. The others marked their own ballots.

A couple of the businessmen of the town came in during the next few minutes and cast their ballots, then there

was a lull in the voting. A frown grew slowly on Miller's
face, but it disappeared a few minutes before eight. Two
or three people came in to vote and at eight o'clock
there was actually a small line waiting to mark their
ballots.

Miller remembered that the *Star* had announced that
the polls would be open from eight to six.

A steady stream of people came in between eight and
nine o'clock and Miller, glancing at the record book,
judged that a hundred people had voted in the first hour.

A few minutes after nine o'clock South Street exploded. Hong Kong Smith's men rode into town in a body
and whooped and yelled in front of the bank where Smith
was getting the money to pay them. There was more
whooping and shooting when the crew went into the Mc-
Coy's Saloon to receive their money and imbibe their
first drinks.

For the next half hour there was only an occasional
burst of noise as a cowboy spewed out of the saloon, but
then there was a sudden rattle of gunfire and Packard,
looking out of the window, suddenly gasped.

"They're coming here!"

Luke Miller left the ballot box and stepped to the window. A swarm of Texas men, led by Hong Kong Smith,
was charging toward the jail.

Lee Kinnaird stepped through the door and found
Chuck Gorey already there. Luke Miller came out behind
him.

"Gonna fulfill our civic duty," Hong Kong Smith
boomed. He saw the sign on the wall. " 'Vote here,' " he
roared.

"You can't vote!" snapped Luke Miller.

"Who says we can't?" cried Hong Kong Smith. He
turned to his cowboys. "He says we can't vote!"

A half dozen guns were discharged into the air and
were scarcely heard above the roar of the Texas men.
They surged forward, pushing Hong Kong Smith against
Lee Kinnaird and Luke Miller. Kinnaird put his hand on
Smith's chest.

"Don't crowd me, Smith," Kinnaird muttered, icily.

Smith's tongue came out and licked his lips. "I got as
much right to vote as anybody." He appealed to Chuck
Gorey. "Ain't that right, Marshal?"

Gorey shot a quick look at Lee Kinnaird.

"Seems I got nothin' to say about it," replied Gorey. "They got a committee of six to say who votes and who don't." He gestured to the group of poll officials, all of whom had come out by now. "Ask them."

"We're asking," said Smith.

"As far as I'm concerned you vote," growled McCoy, the saloonman. He was immediately seconded by Holt and Tobin.

"And we say you don't," declared Luke Miller, indicating Packard and Kinnaird. "Only legitimate residents of Sage City and Sage County can vote."

"What's a legitimate resident?" sneered Hong Kong Smith.

"People who live here."

"How long?"

Miller scowled. The question had never come up. In frontier towns everybody voted, even though they may have arrived only the day before.

"The intent of the law," Miller said, harshly, "is that people vote who have a permanent interest in a community. The length of time they have lived in a place isn't too important. The point is the voter must be a legitimate settler."

"We're settlers," howled Hong Kong Smith. "We're all settlers here, ain't we, boys?"

His men roared in the affirmative. Again there was a forward surge and the committee of six was forced back to the door of the marshal's office. Then Jacob Fugger came through the crowd. He was followed by Horace Van Meter.

"We can hold a council meeting right here, Miller," he said, as he came forward. He pointed to his members on the voting committee. "You're all councilmen. All right, do we let these *settlers* vote, or do we not?"

Miller capitulated. "Save your breath."

Sixty-two Texas men voted in the next half hour. When the crowd in the marshal's office thinned out, Luke Miller left. He walked down South Street to the corner and turned to his shop.

"You'd better go and vote now," he said to Hudkins and Tancred.

"I haven't been in town long enough to vote," Tancred said.

"You've been here longer than the sixty-two Texas men who just voted," snapped Miller.

Tancred whistled softly. "So that's what the noise was about!"

Miller nodded. "We're licked."

"Those sixty-two votes are enough to swing it?"

"About a hundred people voted before they showed up. We were running about fifty percent, maybe a little better. I think we'd have made it, by forty, maybe fifty votes. I figured on a total vote of possibly three hundred and I thought we'd swing about a hundred and seventy, maybe eighty of the total. But now. . . ." He shook his head.

"Have any of the farmers come in yet?"

"What farmers?"

"Quite a few are still around."

"They only come into town when they have to. The Texas men push them around."

"But they're on your side."

A gleam of hope came to Miller's eyes, but then faded. "They're too scattered."

"You were thinking of going after them?"

"Just for a moment. If we had enough men and horses. . . ." He paused. "The livery stable's got a dozen horses or more."

"It's Fugger's livery stable."

"All the better." Miller suddenly chuckled. "Wait here . . . !"

He dashed out of the shop. Tancred went back to his work. Ten minutes later Miller came in, followed by Herb Glassman, Fred Kraft and two other men. "Mose," he shouted. "Quick pull a proof of our subscribers."

While Hudkins was following Miller's instructions, the newspaperman turned to the men he had brought in. "We can't cover them all, but we can reach half of them, I'm sure. Those you talk to can tell the others."

Two more men came into the shop. By that time Hudkins had pulled the proofs of the subscription list. Miller skimmed down the list with a pencil, checking those names he felt sure were farmers.

"I count twenty-nine, but I don't know everyone. There might be that many more. Remember, it doesn't matter how long they've lived here—Fugger settled that. Every man who can come in, can vote. Now, wait a minute, let's not go over to the livery stable in a body . . . one or two at a time. Herb, you and Walter start now." He signalled to Tancred. "How about you, John? Care to ride into the country?"

Tancred took off his shop apron.

Chapter 18

Ten minutes later, astride a rented horse, Tancred rode out of Sage City. He took the south road, but once he passed the last house, he turned to the west and south, cutting across the prairie. His route took him across the grazing grounds of the Texas herds and he soon came upon a herd of more than two thousand longhorns, guarded by a few cowboys.

He skirted the herd, then put his horse into a swift lope that put the distance behind them. Yet he saw no signs of human habitation until he was more than three miles from Sage City. Then a half-buried sod house loomed up before him. It was a miserable house, built of logs and mud, with sod serving for roofing. Behind it was a tiny corral in which stood two work-horses and a single cow.

As Tancred rode up, a man came out of the sod house with a rifle in his hands.

Tancred held up his hand. "Do you read the *Sage City Star?*" he asked the settler.

The man looked at Tancred through slitted, red eyes. "I don't want no trouble. I'm pulling up stakes in a couple of days and I don't want no trouble with anyone."

"I'm not going to make any trouble," Tancred said. "It's just, well, they're having an election in town today and we're asking everybody to come in and vote."

"Vote for who?"

"That's for you to decide. Vote for whoever you please. The main thing is we want you to vote."

"I don't know nothin' about votin'," the man said, dispiritedly. "I'm a farmer. Least I thought I was"—he made a sudden, spiteful gesture with his rifle toward the east—"if those cowboys'd let me. I had a crop of wheat started and they turned their steers loose on it."

"That," said Tancred, "is what the voting's about. Some

of the people in town want to put a stop to things like that. And you can help, by voting."

The man cocked his head to one side. "Nobody cares about us farmers. Everybody calls us squatters."

"A group of people in town sent me out here," Tancred persisted. "They want to put a stop to Jacob Fugger's one-man rule of Sage City and Sage County."

"You mean I could vote *against* Jacob Fugger?" the squatter asked with sudden interest.

"You can!"

"And what'll Fugger do to anyone who votes against him?"

"There's nothing he can do. Besides, he won't know who's voted against him."

Tancred grabbed up his reins. "Think it over. But remember the polls close at six o'clock. Get in town before then if you want to vote."

He touched his heels to the horse's flanks and it bounded away. He looked over his shoulder and the farmer had turned and was looking after him.

It was ten minutes and two miles before Tancred found another squatter on the prairie. The man was a Swede and spoke only broken English, but his wife listened closely and questioned Tancred and before Tancred rode off she said to her husband, "You go and vote!"

By mid-afternoon Tancred had ridden thirty miles, in a wide circle and had found eight farmers. His circle had brought him close to Sage City again and his heaving horse told him that he could not ride much farther.

Ahead, was a herd of Texas' longhorns. He circled to the left and saw that he would pass near a cowboy.

The man was slumped in his saddle. As Tancred came up he glanced idly at him and averted his eyes, but suddenly they darted back to Tancred, in sudden shock.

A shudder ran through Tancred. He pulled up his mount.

"Tancred," said Dave Helm.

The years disappeared. The man facing Tancred had been one of Quantrell's chief lieutenants, had commanded the troop of which Tancred had been a member. They had ridden side by side into Lawrence, at Centralia they had charged the Union cavalry together. At ghastly Westport they had stormed the breastworks of the Kansas militia. And then, after the war, they had ridden with the

now legendary Sam Older. And Dave Helm—Dave Helm
had been present when Tancred and Sam Older had faced
each other in that crashing finale!

Tancred said, "Hello, Dave."

Dave Helm exhaled heavily. "It's been a long time,
Wes." He shook his head. "How have things been with
you?"

"Not good," Tancred replied, steadily. He gestured to
the herd. "You're a cowboy?"

Helm shrugged. "Texas seemed like a good place, back
in 'sixty-seven. I haven't been north until now."

"This is one of Hong Kong Smith's herds?"

"I work on his home ranch. You, Wes?"

"I haven't stayed very long in one place."

"I've heard a lot about you." Helm grimaced. "That
damn song, they sing it all the time down in Texas. Made
things kind of rough for you, hasn't it?"

Tancred made no reply for a moment. Then he asked,
quietly, "What about you, Dave?"

"What about me?" Then Helm exclaimed. "Hey, you
mean about that song? Hell, man, I was there when you
downed Sam Older. Older was about the orneriest man
who ever lived. The song . . ." He wrinkled his nose in
disgust. "Try to tell someone it ain't true and they look at
you as if you were crazy." He chuckled. "I tried it a couple—three years ago. Told the fella I was Dave Helm.
He'd never even heard of me. Just Sam Older . . . and
you."

"What's become of Dick Small?"

"I had a letter from him four-five years ago. He was
running a grocery store over in Arkansas. Don't know
what happened to Fletch McCorkle. I was never very
friendly with him. Like I said, I stayed down in Texas.
Wouldn't be here now if old Hong Kong hadn't sent for
me. Somebody's been giving a friend of his some trouble. . . ." He stopped, his eyes narrowing. "You live
here, Wes?"

"I've been here for a little while."

A perplexed frown settled upon Helm's features. "They
know who you are?"

"No. I've used a different name since . . . since 'sixty-
seven."

"The name wouldn't be . . . Bailey?"

Tancred nodded.

"I should have known!" exclaimed Helm. "Smith said you'd killed three men with just three bullets at a place near here . . ." Then he suddenly winced. "But you're not wearing a gun."

"I never carry one," said Tancred evenly. "I work as a printer."

"You—a printer!"

"If you'll think back, you'll remember that's what I was doing in Lexington when I first joined up with Sam Older."

"Yeah, sure, I'd forgotten." He grinned. "Nobody would suspect that Wes Tancred was a printer." A cloud came over his face again. "Texas is a big place, but it's not big enough to hide from Hong Kong Smith. They consider him a hero down there. He's given the ranchers the only hard money they've known since the war." He looked thoughtfully at Tancred. "By now you've guessed why Smith brought me up here."

"Me?"

Helm nodded. "Funny, isn't it?"

"Fugger's already brought in Eric Stratemeyer."

Helm whistled. "I've heard of him, even down in Texas."

"And there's a Texas man named Manny Harpending."

"Not in your class."

"Neither Harpending or Stratemeyer—or you, Dave— will make me take up a gun. I haven't carried one since the time of Sam Older."

"But the three men at that stage station here . . . or was that poppycock?"

"That was . . . one of those things. It won't happen again."

"You're sure, Wes? Nothing could make you take up a gun?"

"I can't think of anything that could."

Dave Helm showed relief. "I'm glad to hear that. I— I'd hate to think of facing you across a gun. And I don't mean that just because you happen to be good with a gun. You know that, Wes."

"I know it."

"It's because of . . . well, the past, Wes." He hesitated and the frown came again to his face. "I never came in, Wes. I'm wanted in Missouri and—yes, in Kansas, too.

I'm only safe in Texas and I'm not safe there if Hong Kong Smith is against me."

"So you'll take your orders from Smith?"

"I've got to."

"You'll tell him who I am?"

"I don't know the setup. He told me not to come into town today. Until they knew how an election was going."

"It may go against Smith—rather Fugger, who's on Smith's team."

Helm groaned. "That makes a hard choice."

Tancred picked up the reins of his mount. "Good-bye, Dave."

"Good-bye."

Tancred rode on.

Tancred re-entered Sage City shortly before four o'clock. Luke Miller, standing outside the courthouse, saw him ride up the street and signalling to him, came out into the street.

"Fred Kraft's back and Walter Colmes rode in just a few minutes ago. They said some people were coming in."

"I talked to a few and got some promises from some of them."

"Then where are they?" exclaimed Miller. "Only two farmers that I know of have come in to vote."

"There's still two hours."

"Most of the townspeople have voted. There's been quite a turnout, but I can tell you right now that we're still behind at least twenty-five or thirty votes."

"Do you want me to go out again?"

"Would it be any use?"

"I saw only eight people in my circle. I may have missed one or two, but not more."

Miller said, wearily, "Turn back your horse to the livery stable. Then come and vote. We may as well have that vote."

Tancred rode his mount to the livery stable and received a black look from the attendant. "You'd never have got this horse if I'd known what you were going to use it for."

"It's a good horse," said Tancred. "If you were going to sell it, what would you ask for it?"

"More money than you've got."

"How much?"

The man hesitated. "What do you want to buy a horse for?"

"Because I like this horse."

"Do you like it a hundred dollars' worth?"

"I might."

Tancred turned away. Out on the street he stopped. In spite of the fact that the town was filled with Texas men, there wasn't as much noise and commotion as there usually was.

He crossed to the Bon Ton Café, remembering that he had not eaten since morning. When he came out it was a quarter to five. He looked toward the courthouse, then recrossed the street and entered the Texas Saloon.

The place was crowded. A good deal of drinking was going on and some Texas men were wrangling among themselves, but it was not an unruly crowd.

He found a place at the far end of the bar, near Lily's office and ordered a glass of beer. He noted that the office door was partially opened and carrying his beer he went to it. He knocked.

"Yes?" called Lily from inside.

"John Bailey."

There was a pause, then she opened the door. "Come in."

He went in and she closed the door. "Have you performed your civic duty of voting?" she asked. "Isn't that what Hong Kong Smith called it?"

"I wasn't there, but I heard that he voted—along with sixty-some Texas men."

"It didn't surprise you that Jacob Fugger had an ace up his sleeve?"

"He's got a packful of aces," Tancred said. "Including one that he doesn't know about yet."

Lily looked at him in mock surprise. "Well! What do you know?" Then, as he looked at her inquiringly, "You, you actually said something that I didn't have to pull out of you."

"That bothers you."

She became serious. "Yes . . . things about you bother me. And I hate myself that they do." She looked at him boldly. "You know, don't you?"

He was silent and she exclaimed bitterly, "That drove you right back into your shell."

"Don't, Lily!"

"All right, all right," she said, forcing the usual note of asperity into her tone. "I'll put on a new face and go out there and sing for the boys. They've got to be entertained so they'll stay here and spend their money instead of going to one of the other saloons on the street."

"What are you going to sing, Lily?" Tancred asked, dully.

In the act of turning away from him she whirled and stared at him. Then she came closer. "John," she said, slowly, "there's something on your mind—something you want to tell me." She paused. "I—I have a suspicion as to what it is—it's—about that song?"

"I think you know."

"I've seen your face while I sang it and I . . . I've been thinking about you. The Turkey Crossing affair . . . your marksmanship against Wild Bill Hickok."

"Yes," he said, "I'm Wes Tancred."

She stared at him wide-eyed.

"I started to tell you about the ace in the hole that Fugger's got and doesn't know about—yet. That's it. I ran into Dave Helm. Hong Kong Smith sent for him—to kill me."

"Dave Helm was one of Sam Older's men!"

He nodded. "We were friends in the old days. But Dave Helm . . . is Dave Helm. He works for Smith."

"What are you going to do, Wes?"

"What can I do? Run . . ."

"I think you've done quite a lot of running in your time."

"Who would it help if I stayed? If Miller loses the election he's through. If he wins and it came out that Wes Tancred was working for him, it would hurt him."

"I sang that song to you," Lily said.

"You didn't know."

"Not the first time, but I sang it again when—well, maybe I didn't know, but I sang it deliberately, because I knew it hurt you, somehow."

"I've listened to the song before, Lily—a great many times. You can get used to a lot of things. You get a thick skin."

"You, Wes? You're telling me now that you have a thick skin?" She gripped his arm, savagely. "I said I was quitting in four years. I don't have to wait four years.

I've got enough—now. I can sell this place or I can just close it up and go with you."

"No, Lily," he said gently. "I've ridden alone too long."

She let go of his arm and the light went out of her eyes. "It's that girl, Laura Vesser. She's not your kind, Wes. She's—too fragile . . ."

A heavy fist banged on the office door and a hoarse voice shouted, "Miss Lily—come out and see what's happening."

Lily exclaimed in sudden anger, but stepped past Tancred and pulled open the door. "What is it?" she cried to the bartender who had knocked on the door.

"It's outside, there's about a thousand farmers come into town . . . they're going to vote!"

Lily whirled on Tancred. "You knew?"

"I spent several hours riding around, talking to some of them. And so did some other people on Miller's side. I thought they weren't going to show up, but they did."

He started to go out, then stopped. Her eyes met his.

"This is it?"

"I won't be here tomorrow."

The door was open and in the saloon proper a stream of men were pouring toward the front door. Lily laughed. "All right, then." He nodded and went out. After a moment she followed.

When Tancred reached the street, some of the farmers had already gone into the marshal's office, but at least twenty-five or thirty were outside, some on horses, some in farm wagons. All were armed. They were quiet, but their eyes were defiant as they faced the crowds that had poured out of saloons on both sides of the street.

Tancred pushed through the crowd of Texas men and townspeople and crossed to the farmers. He recognized one of the men as one he had spoken to that afternoon.

"We didn't think it was healthy to come in one by one," the man told Tancred. "We met outside of town and came in in a body."

"How many of you are there?"

"We counted before we come in. Forty-eight. And we're all voting the same."

Chapter 19

Luke Miller came into the print shop a few minutes before seven and found Tancred sitting on the cot.

"We won!" exulted Miller. "We won by twenty-seven votes. The farmers did the trick. Tomorrow there'll be a new council, a new sheriff, a new judge. . . ."

"And a new mayor."

"And a new mayor!" Miller clapped Tancred on the shoulder. "There are going to be some changes in Sage City. It isn't going to be Jacob Fugger's private town any more. I've got to go home now. We're having a meeting later. I just stopped in to tell you that we'd won, although I guess you already knew it."

"I figured you were in when I saw the farmers."

Miller starting off, stopped. "By the way, I don't think I saw you vote."

"I didn't. When I got ready there was too much of a crowd there."

"That's a fine business. You go out to bring in the voters and you don't vote yourself," Miller chuckled. "Well, your vote wasn't needed, as it turned out, but don't let any of our friends know you didn't vote."

"I won't," Tancred said.

Miller left the print shop and Tancred, drawing a deep breath, stood and drew out his carpetbag from under the cot. He stepped to the wall and took down his coat from the nail on which it hung. He put it on and without looking back left the shop.

It was almost dark outside and no one paid any attention to Tancred as he walked to the livery stable. He entered and found the attendant forking hay for the horses.

"Here's that hundred dollars," he said.

The man's mouth fell open. "What hundred dollars?"

"The price of that horse," said Tancred, pointing. "That's what you told me it was this afternoon."

The liveryman backed away. "I wasn't counting on selling any horse, not to you."

"You said a hundred dollars," Tancred pursued. "That's more than the horse is worth, but I'm paying you what you asked. And here's twenty-five dollars for a saddle—any saddle you've got in the place."

The man hesitated, then suddenly shrugging, got a saddle and went into the stall. Ten minutes later, his carpetbag dangling from the saddle horn, Tancred rode down the street.

The cowboys, having been held in all day, were cutting loose. They reeled up and down the sidewalks, churned into the streets. They shouted and cursed and sang bawdy songs and fired their guns at the sky, and at store windows.

Tancred was oblivious. He was astride a horse and no one singled him out for attack or abuse. He rode north to the railroad tracks, crossed and rode down the street, past the house where Laura Vesser lived. He did not see her, did not glance at the house as he went by.

Hunched down in the saddle he rode out of Sage City.

Dave Helm had lived so long in Texas he had gotten out of the habit of walking. Luke Miller lived less than two blocks from Fugger's Store where he had received his instructions and his directions, but Helm mounted his horse outside the store and walked it down South Street, then right, past the *Star* printing office and, counting, to the fifth house on the right.

It was a square little house of no more than three rooms. It was nicely painted and reminded Helm of the houses in Missouri that were so unlike the Texas homes . . . and which he had not seen for so many years.

Helm dismounted in front of the house and stepping on the little veranda that was raised a few inches from the ground, knocked on the door.

A man opened the door and looked inquiringly at him.

"Is this the residence of Mayor Miller?" Helm asked, politely.

"I'm Luke Miller, yes," was the reply.

"I'm sorry, Mr. Miller," Helm said. "There's nothing personal about this. It's a job of work, that's all."

He drew his revolver. Shock hit Miller. "No!" he cried, hoarsely. "Don't . . . please don't. . . ."

Helm raised the revolver and fired.

Miller fell back, his head and shoulders landing inside the house. Mrs. Miller, who had heard her husband cry out, screamed and rushed forward.

Helm exhaled wearily and putting away his revolver walked stiffly to his horse. He mounted it and turning, rode back to Fugger's Store.

He tied his horse to the hitchrail and crossing the sidewalk, knocked on the locked door. It was opened after a moment by Hong Kong Smith. Jacob Fugger, who had been hovering back, came forward.

"It's done," said Dave Helm.

Hong Kong Smith took out a huge white handkerchief from his breast pocket and mopped his perspiring forehead. He looked at Jacob Fugger.

"Satisfied?"

"He wouldn't have it any other way," Fugger said, defensively. "He kept crowding me all the time. He wouldn't stop, he kept after me. I didn't want to kill him. . . ."

"Oh, shut up," said Hong Kong Smith. He gestured to Dave Helm. "Come on, let's you and me get drunk."

"I don't touch the stuff," said Helm, morosely. But as Smith turned away, he added quickly, "Well, maybe one drink tonight."

He followed Hong Kong Smith out of Fugger's Store. On the sidewalk Smith started to pass the Texas Saloon, intending to go on to McCoy's Saloon, but a sudden impulse caused him to turn and go into Lily Leeds' place.

The Texas Saloon was more crowded than it had ever been in its four years' existence. They were standing two and three deep at the bar, but Smith grabbed a man by the arm and whirled him away. Another man he elbowed aside. And once he reached the bar he used his huge bulk to shove a space clear for Dave Helm.

A bartender, about to draw a beer for another patron, came over. "Yes, Mr. Smith?"

"Two glasses," said Smith, "and two bottles,"

From another man there would have been a protest over the order, but they all knew Hong Kong Smith and the bartender promptly put two glasses and two bottles before Smith.

"Drink up," Smith said to Dave Helm.

Helm filled his glass and tossed it off in a single gulp. He sputtered and choked as the fiery liquid burned its

way down his gullet and Hong Kong Smith giving him a
hard crack between the shoulder blades only caused
Helm to choke more. When he finally was able to control
the coughing, Smith thrust a second glass into Helm's
hand.

"Drink it slow, this time," he ordered. "It tastes better
that way."

Helm sipped at the whiskey and a warm glow spread
through him. The dullness slipped away and Helm had a
third drink. He drank the last of it and then Lily Leeds
stepped up on the little platform and began to sing.

She sang the song of Sam Older and Wes Tancred and
there was a catch in her voice and a huskiness that had
never been there before and men in the room became
silent and listened. A man stopped whirling the chuck-a-
luck cage and a faro dealer covered his box with his
hands and stared at the layout before him.

At the bar, Dave Helm listened to the song and the
knuckles of his hand whitened as his fingers closed about
the glass in his fist and finally the glass collapsed and he
let the broken pieces fall to the floor. His hand was wet
with whiskey and blood and the whiskey burned into the
cuts, but Helm scarcely felt it. His eyes were on Lily
Leeds.

Lily finished the song and for a moment there was a
dead silence in the crowded saloon. Then a man clapped
and the others took it up until the room vibrated from
the concussion. Lily, her face taut, her eyes stony, walked
through the room to her office. She put her hand on the
door to go in and could not. She couldn't go into the
little room where Wes Tancred had revealed himself that
afternoon. She could not go into the room . . . alone.

She turned to the bar.

Hong Kong Smith, who had drunk three times as much
whiskey as Dave Helm, boomed, "Mighty good singing,
Lily girl, mighty good."

Lily looked at the strained face and the piercing eyes
of Dave Helm, which were on her. "You didn't like it?"

"I liked your singing, ma'am," replied Dave Helm. "I
didn't like the song."

Lily stared at him. "Someone else told me that." Her
eyes fell to Dave's hand. "You're bleeding!"

Helm opened his hand and looked at the blood on his palm. "It's nothing, ma'am, just a little cut."

Lily's eyes dropped to the floor, saw the little shards of glass. Her eyes came up to meet Helm's once more. "Why don't you like the song?"

"'Cause it ain't true, ma'am," Helm said, simply. "Sam Older was never no hero and Wes Tancred wasn't any coward. The song is a lie, ma'am!"

"You," said Lily Leeds, "are Dave Helm."

He made an odd little bow.

"You know him," Lily said. "You talked to him today."

"Wes Tancred, ma'am? Why, yes, he came along this afternoon when I was ridin' herd and we had a little talk."

Hong Kong Smith's huge right hand reached out and struck Helm's shoulder. "Who's that you're talkin' about? Wes Tancred . . . ?"

Helm wrenched his shoulder free of Smith's grip and faced his employer, a spot of color on each cheek. "Don't do that again, Mr. Smith!" he said, softly.

"This Tancred you're talking about," cried Smith. "You know him. He's here in Sage City?"

"Why, yes!"

"I'll be goddamned!" roared Hong Kong Smith.

Lee Kinnaird came along the bar. He was coatless and a star was pinned on the left side of his shirt. His face was sober, his eyes like those of an eagle, searching for prey.

He came up to the group and said, "Luke Miller was killed fifteen minutes ago."

"Oh, no!" gasped Lily. "Fugger wouldn't dare."

"He dared all right."

Hong Kong Smith pointed a thick forefinger at the star on Kinnaird's chest. "You didn't waste any time pinning that on."

Kinnaird said, "Fugger himself hasn't got the guts to kill a prairie dog and Eric Stratemeyer was in McCoy's all evening, so it was one of your hellions who did the job."

"Maybe," sneered Smith, "then again maybe it was your friend, what's he been calling himself?—Bailey. Shooting people when they ain't looking's in his line." He stopped, as Kinnaird's eyes bored into him. "Or maybe you didn't know your fine friend was the dirty coward, Wes Tancred."

"So that's why he's left town!"

"What?" cried Smith. "He's run out? That proves his guilt."

"It proves only that he's gone," retorted Kinnaird. "Mrs. Miller saw the killer. It wasn't," he continued firmly, "John Bailey."

Laura Vesser was in bed, but not asleep when Mrs. Martin knocked on her door.

"Yes?" Laura called.

Mrs. Martin opened the door far enough to poke in her head. "I didn't know if you were awake or not. I—I thought you might want to know—Mr. Miller, the newspaper publisher, has been killed."

Laura cried out in dismay. She threw back the bedcovers and swung her feet to the floor. "How—how was he killed?" she asked, fearfully.

"I don't know rightly. Mrs. Miller told the sheriff that someone knocked on their door and when Mr. Miller went to answer it, he was shot down without a word. But there's talk that a man working for him did the shooting. . . ."

Laura's hand flew to her mouth to shut off a low cry that was torn from her throat. "Not—John Bailey!"

"That's the one. He's been in the store. Only now they say that his name isn't really Bailey—it's Tancred, the notorious murderer."

"Wes Tancred isn't a murderer!"

Mrs. Martin let the bedroom door swing open in her astonishment. "You knew he was this man Tancred?"

"I knew him before I came to Sage City. I knew him . . . a long time."

Chapter 20

A half hour after Fugger's Store opened in the morning, Kinnaird came in. Laura was waiting on a customer and he stopped by the door and pretended to be examining some Levi's, until Laura had finished with her customer. He approached her then.

"You've heard?"

She nodded.

"What do you think?"

"It's not true—about Wes, I mean."

"Wes?"

"Of course. That's his name, Wes."

"I see," said Kinnaird, dully. "You've known who he was all along? Before you both came to Sage City?"

"Yes."

"You agreed at Turkey Crossing to come here."

"Oh, no. It wasn't like that. . . ." Laura looked at the sheriff in astonishment. "No, Lee. He told me who he was before he rode off, but that—that's all." Pain came into her eyes. "There was nothing between us, Lee."

"I suppose not," said Kinnaird. "Not if you say so, Laura. Only . . ." He shook his head. "I liked him." He looked at her, thoughtfully, a little worry creasing his forehead. "You, Laura?"

"What do you mean?" she asked, disconcerted.

"You liked him? Or perhaps it's more than just liking him."

"Oh, no!"

The quickness of her reply did not relieve Kinnaird. He sighed wearily. "I don't think he should have left town."

"But why not? He didn't do it, but because of his—his past, they'd accuse him of it."

"Oh, that's just talk. If it came right down to it, nobody could make that stick. Fugger's trying to, to cover

116

himself." He shot a quick glance at the balcony. "It isn't that. It's just . . . well, Miller counted on him. That's one of the reasons he got so tough with Fugger. He figured Tancred would back him up and he didn't."

"No, Lee," said Laura in dismay. "You're wrong. I know you're wrong. Mr. Miller didn't know who he was. I'm sure of that. He—he's not like that at all. He doesn't *want* to fight. He never carries a gun, even—"

"He had one at Turkey Crossing!"

"No, he didn't. I mean, he didn't carry it. Please—I was there. Father tried to get him to do something about the—the men beforehand. Wes wouldn't, tried to talk Father out of going against them. But Father wouldn't listen. He'd hidden this gun and then—then he ran out with it and before anyone could stop him—he was dead. It was *then* Wes shot them. He didn't pick the fight."

"That sounds just like here," Kinnaird said. "He wouldn't carry a gun, he wouldn't fight. But Miller knew who he was and counted on him."

"Father *didn't* know who he was! That's the point, Lee. For all Father knew Wes was just a man who took care of the horses . . . a sick man. I—he told me after it was all over who he was. That was when I . . ."

She winced and stopped.

"All right," Kinnaird said. He shot another look at the balcony, shook his head and went off.

After the door had closed behind him, Fugger poked open a little window on the balcony and called down, "Laura! Come up here."

Laura climbed the stairs and entered Fugger's office. "Yes, Mr. Fugger."

"I saw Kinnaird down there talking to you. What did he want?"

"Why—why nothing, Mr. Fugger!"

Fugger made an angry gesture. "Rubbish! You were leaning toward each other like a—a couple of love birds."

Laura gasped. "Mr. Fugger!"

"Don't Mister Fugger me," shouted Jacob. "What were you talking about down there, on *my* time?"

Laura drew herself together. "We were talking about—about what happened last night."

"About this Tancred fellow killing the newspaper-man?" sneered Fugger. "Another one of your fine friends, this Tancred. I must say you know how to pick them."

"If you're through, I'll get back to my work," Laura said, with sudden dignity.

"I'll tell you when I'm through! You forget that you're working for me. And you'll work in this town if *I* want you to work. If I discharge you for—for impertinence—there isn't another man in town who'd employ you. He wouldn't dare."

"I know that, Mr. Fugger." Laura nodded coolly and turning, started for the stairs.

Jacob Fugger opened his mouth to pour another blast after her, but changed his mind. He leaned forward, so he could watch through the little window.

He saw Laura walking stiffly down the stairs, saw how she held her head erect, saw the rise and fall of her bosom. A slow flush crept over his face. His tongue came out and moistened his lips.

Hong Kong Smith drank through the night. Once he slept for a half hour with his face on the table, but he awakened when a drunken cowboy bumped into the table. He knocked the man down with his fist and catching up a bottle from the table, put it to his mouth and took a copious swallow of the whiskey.

By morning Smith was stupid from liquor. McCoy tried to talk him into going to the hotel and get some sleep, but Smith threw the bottle at him. McCoy sent out for a big order of ham and eggs and put the food on the table before him. Smith wolfed down the food and demanded another order. It was brought to him and he ate it, then he had a couple more drinks and was able to get to his feet.

"This place stinks," he shouted. "Why don't you ever air it out?"

"The door's open now," McCoy pointed out.

Smith dragged a chair to the door, pushed through the batwings and planted his chair on the sidewalk directly in front of the door. He sat down heavily.

"Bring me a bottle!" he roared.

McCoy did not come with the bottle immediately and Smith dragged a long-barreled revolver from under his coat and fired at the batwing doors. The bullet tore through the flimsy wood and missed McCoy, hurrying forward, by inches.

McCoy charged through the door.

"You're going too far, Smith!" he said, angrily.

"What's that, you damnyank? Why, I'll buy your damn saloon and burn it to the ground."

McCoy made a tremendous effort to control himself. He handed the bottle of whiskey to Smith. "Here's your bottle!" He went back into the saloon.

Hong Kong Smith tilted the bottle to his mouth and drank deeply. Then he lowered the bottle and looked owlishly across the street. His eyes focused on the wooden sign over the Boston Store and he raised his revolver. Sighting drunkenly he fired. The bullet missed the sign by about ten feet, going off into space.

"Too high," muttered Smith. He depressed the revolver, took aim and fired again. Glass crashed as the bullet went through the window.

He was aiming a third time at the sign, when Gil Packard dashed out of the store. He saw Hong Kong Smith across the street and threw himself to the sidewalk. Smith fired a third time and again glass shattered, but it was the window of the Bon Ton Café this time.

"Lousy gun's no good," growled Hong Kong Smith.

He aimed again, but the sign of the Boston Store seemed to elude him and he swung the gun around and brought it to bear upon the window of the bank. He gripped his right hand with his left and holding it reasonably steady, pulled the trigger. The bullet crashed through the window of the bank.

Lee Kinnaird, who had heard the shooting, while he was inside the sheriff's office, came out on the street. Swearing under his breath, he started across the street. As he reached the side where Smith was, the Texan fired a fifth time. The bullet missed Kinnaird by inches and hit the courthouse.

Kinnaird ran forward and grabbed the gun in Smith's hand.

"What do you think you're doing, you drunken fool?" he cried.

He tried to jerk the gun from Smith's hand, but the big man held on to it with drunken strength.

"Lemme 'lone," he muttered. He jerked the gun free of Kinnaird's grip and swung the muzzle to point at Kinnaird. The latter, not knowing that the gun was empty, whipped out his own revolver and springing forward, smashed the barrel along the side of Smith's head.

Hong Kong Smith went over backward, rolling to the sidewalk. The blow that Kinnaird struck him was a hard one and Smith, rolling over, groaned and lapsed into unconsciousness. Angrily, Kinnaird stooped and jerked up Smith. He let the big man fall forward over his shoulder and grunting from the weight of him, carried him across the street, to the courthouse.

Gorey looked up as Kinnaird came in carrying the huge Texan.

"Who you got there?" he demanded, then recognized him. "Hong Kong Smith! What're you doing with him?"

"I'm putting him in jail."

"You can't! Not him. . . ."

Kinnaird carried the big man into the cell behind the marshal's office and dumped him onto a cot. Gorey came in after him. "There'll be trouble over this."

"He's made it," snapped Kinnaird. "The drunken fool was firing that gun all around. Almost hit me."

"That was here in town," protested Gorey. "I'm the marshal and you got no right—"

"As sheriff I've got the right to arrest a man anywhere in the county. Especially if the marshal of a town is no damn good!"

Gorey glowered at Kinnaird, but uncertain of his ground, decided to appeal to a higher authority. He left the couthouse and went to ask Jacob Fugger. But that worthy had already been informed of what had happened and was coming toward the courthouse.

He encountered Kinnaird coming out. "You can't arrest Hong Kong Smith," he cried.

"Maybe I can't," said Kinnaird, grimly, "but I did."

"Turn him loose!"

"He's unconscious. I had to crack him over the head."

Fugger cried out in horror. "There'll be trouble over this."

"For Smith. When he sobers up I'm taking him before the judge."

Fugger brightened for an instant, but then looked suspiciously at Kinnaird.

"What judge?"

"The only judge in the county—Judge Kraft!"

Fugger winced. "Kinnaird, I'll give you ten minutes to cool off. Then I'll be back."

"Better come with a gun," warned Kinnaird.

Fugger whirled away. He went straight to McCoy's Saloon. McCoy was bitter about Smith. "He took a shot at me."

"He didn't hit you."

"It wasn't his fault that he didn't. I saw the whole thing. He put a bullet through the bank window, among other things."

Fugger grimaced. "We've got to overlook what he's done. We—we need him and his business."

"I suppose we do, but how far can we let a man go?"

"He's never been this drunk before."

"His men have, plenty of them."

Fugger suddenly bared his teeth. "I'm not going to argue with you, McCoy. The point is, we've got to get him out of jail. When he sobers up and finds what's been done to him, there'll be trouble. He's a vindictive man." He looked around. "Where's Eric Stratemeyer?"

McCoy looked toward a room at the rear. "Sleeping."

"Wake him up."

"You're not going to send him against Kinnaird?"

"Not if I don't have to. Kinnaird's being unreasonable about the whole thing."

McCoy hesitated but went toward the office at the rear. He found Stratemeyer awake. "What's all the racket about?" the faro dealer asked.

"Hong Kong Smith's been shooting up the place," McCoy said. "The sheriff conked him and threw him in the calaboose and Fugger's outside now. He—he wants to talk to you."

Stratemeyer shrugged and put on his coat. He followed McCoy into the saloon.

"You," said Fugger. "I want you to go down to the jail and get Hong Kong Smith out."

Stratemeyer fixed Fugger with a cold look. "I haven't had much experience breaking people out of jail."

"Now, don't *you* go making trouble," Fugger complained. "I've had enough these last few days. I brought you here to town—"

"Let's get things straight," Stratemeyer said. "You sent for me to do one particular job—get rid of a man named

Bailey. He's skipped town. Maybe I scared him out, maybe I didn't."

"I'm not worried about that now."

"All right, you've got another job? You'll pay me a thousand dollars?"

Fugger swallowed hard. "You drive a hard bargain."

"They tell me you do, too," retorted Stratemeyer. "You want me to gun the sheriff?"

Fugger hesitated. "I'll let you know later."

"You do that, Mr. Fugger. In the meantime, would you mind sending over the thousand dollars you already owe me?" Stratemeyer smiled, a cold smile that sent a chill running through Fugger. He nodded and virtually ran out of the saloon.

On the street he encountered Manny Harpending and three or four Texas men. "Harpending," Fugger called. "If you're looking for your boss, he's in jail."

"I just heard that," exclaimed Harpending. "Who—who had the nerve to do that?"

"The sheriff. I asked him to turn Smith loose, but he said no Texas men could take Smith away from him."

"How about that, boys?" asked Harpending, appealing to his fellow Texans.

"We'll see about that!" cried one of the Texans.

"Mr. Smith's my best friend," Fugger pursued. "I don't think it's right that a man should hit him over the head with a gun, then drag him over to prison and say he's going to take him before the judge . . . a judge that happens to hate all Texas men. . . ."

Inside of twenty minutes, a score or more of Texas men marched on the jail. Kinnaird, pale but determined, met them at the door.

"Don't do anything foolish, men," he warned the Texas men.

"We're gonna take your jail apart if you don't turn old Hong Kong loose in thirty seconds," shouted one of the Texas men.

Kinnaird drew his gun. He was ready to make an issue of it and then Marshal Gorey appeared appeared in the doorway behind him. Kinnaird, hearing his step, started to turn and a Texas man close by sprang upon Kinnaird and smashed him on the head with his gun.

A roar went up and the Texans charged the jail, trampling and kicking Kinnaird as they swarmed over him. Gorey made no resistance and inside of a minute, Hong Kong Smith, only half-conscious, was brought out.

The mob paid no attention to Kinnaird, but when they left the jail, Kinnaird picked himself up, bleeding and bruised.

Tancred rode steadily through the night, until nearly dawn, when he stopped and staked out his horse on the prairie. Using his carpetbag for a pillow he stretched out on the buffalo grass and was asleep within a few minutes.

He awakened a few hours later and was soon in the saddle. He rode steadily all that day to the east and north and the following morning cut the stage trail. He followed it until late afternoon, when he crossed a shallow stream and sighted the stage station at Turkey Crossing.

The station attendant and his wife, a middle-aged couple, both came out of the station.

"Could I get something to eat?" Tancred asked.

"We was just going to have our supper," replied the attendant's wife. "You're welcome to sit down with us."

"And something for my horse?"

"I'll help you take care of him," volunteered the station agent.

Tancred unsaddled the horse and turned it into the corral with the stage-line animals. He rubbed the horse down with a handful of hay while the agent brought a measure of oats.

"You'll be riding on after supper?" the agent asked.

"I'd like to rest here, if you don't mind."

"There's plenty of room in the barn," was the reply, "and we don't see people here very often. Just twice a week."

"I know," said Tancred.

The agent looked sharply at him.

The supper was a plain one, but substantial, and Tancred, who had not eaten for two days, was grateful for it. When he had finished eating he walked outside and, after a moment, found himself heading for the little mound of earth, back of the station, that contained the remains of Laura Vesser's father.

He stood there for a few minutes and when he turned away he saw the agent, standing some fifty feet away, watching him.

"You knew him?" asked the man.

Tancred nodded. "He was a good man."

"That's what they told me. But me, I don't even keep a gun. Ain't nothing of value here but the horses and the company says I don't have to risk my life to keep them."

Chapter 21

Kinnaird, a bandage about his head and showing several cuts and bruises on his face, stood outside Fugger's Store as Laura Vesser came out a minute or two after twelve.

She exclaimed when she saw his face. "You're hurt!"

Kinnaird made a gesture of dismissal. "I was a hero this morning . . . almost." He took her arm. "I'll buy your lunch."

She flashed him a smile. "I've only a half hour."

"It'll be enough." He steered her toward the Texas Saloon, but as they got to the door, Laura pulled back. "I can't go in here."

"Nobody'll bother you," said Kinnaird.

"Couldn't we eat at the Bon Ton Café?"

"They've sent over some food. There's a—a friend here, wants to talk to you."

Dubiously, Laura allowed herself to be led into the Texas Saloon. As they walked through toward Lily Leeds' office in the rear, a whistle or two went up. Laura, keeping her eyes on the floor, flushed.

Lily Leeds was standing in the door of her office. She backed in. "How are you, Miss Vesser? I'm Lily Leeds."

A table had been set up inside the office, with chairs for three. Food was already on the table. Kinnaird closed the door. "How's this for service?"

"It's very nice," murmured Laura.

"Sit down," said Lily. "We'll eat while we talk."

Kinnaird pulled out a chair and Laura sat down. Lily and Kinnaird also seated themselves and began to eat, but Laura fidgeted with her food. She looked up suddenly and found Lily's eyes on her.

"I . . . Lee said you wanted to talk to me," Laura said, in some confusion.

"I wanted to meet you," declared Lily. "I've heard so much of you that I wanted to see what you were like."

125

"I don't understand," Laura said. "Who . . . ?" Then she looked at Kinnaird.

He shook his head. "Not me." He paused. "Wes."

Laura looked at Lily in astonishment. "Wes talked to you . . . about me?"

"Not exactly. He doesn't talk much—at least not to me. But he came in here before he left and told me he was going. I knew it was because of you."

Laura's eyes clouded. "Why should he leave town because of me?"

"Because he's in love with you."

Laura's hand twitched suddenly and she knocked over her cup of coffee. In the confusion of clearing up, she recovered herself. But if she thought Lily would be distracted by the incident, she was mistaken.

Lily said, "You see, I offered to go with him and he turned me down."

And then Laura felt the coldness that she had not known she possessed, until that morning when Fugger had gone too far, sweep over her once more.

"I don't believe I care to discuss that particular subject."

A look of grudging admiration came over Kinnaird's face. But Lily's eyes narrowed. "Where's he gone to?"

"Didn't he tell you where he was going?"

"No, he didn't."

Laura pushed back her chair. "I've got to get back to work."

"Just a moment," exclaimed Lily. "That fine employer of yours has been accusing Wes Tancred of killing the mayor and first thing you know he'll be sending out a warrant for his arrest."

"Not through me," said Kinnaird.

"He doesn't have to go through you, you know that as well as I. I want to warn Wes."

"I've got to go," said Laura, firmly. She started for the door.

Kinnaird grinned at the furious Lily as Laura went out. "Next time," he said, "you'll let me in on things."

"Don't be stupid, Lee," snapped Lily.

"You told me you just wanted to meet her. And then it turned out to be a cat fight."

"She's in love with him."

Kinnaird sobered. "But he's run out on her."

"No, he hasn't. She knows where he is. She's going to meet him later."

"I doubt that."

"Don't keep your fingers crossed. She can't see you, Lee. Not as long as there's Tancred."

Kinnaird said, harshly, "Maybe not, but *he* can't see *you* as long as she's around."

He went out.

When Laura returned to the store, Mrs. Martin got her shawl. "Hasn't been a customer in twenty minutes," she said. "I'll get something to eat."

She went out and Laura went to her counter. The other clerk was apparently out in the storeroom at the back of the store and she was alone in the store.

She looked up toward the balcony and gave a start. The little window was open and Jacob Fugger was looking down at her. He called, "Laura, come up a minute."

Frowning, Laura crossed to the stairs and climbed up. Fugger was standing by his desk, as she entered the office.

"Close the door," he ordered.

"There's no one in the store," Laura countered. "I want to listen for the door."

"Close it!" he snapped.

She closed the door and turned to find his vulture eyes boring at her.

He said, "You're a very pretty young woman, Laura."

She flushed. "Thank you, Mr. Fugger."

"Call me Jacob, when we're alone." His tongue darted out and flicked his upper lip. "A man like me could do a lot for a woman like you." He took a step forward and Laura said, desperately:

"I think I heard someone come in the store!"

Fugger sent an angry look through the little window, down into the store. "There's no one come in." He reached toward her, saw that his hand trembled and suddenly lunged for her.

"Damn you," he panted. "You drive a man crazy." He grabbed her arm, pulled her toward him.

"Mr. Fugger!" cried Laura. "Don't. . . ."

He wrestled her into his arms. "Throw yourself at a damn killer like Tancred, but a man like me . . . a rich man who could do things. . . ."

Laura struggled furiously to get out of his stringy

arms, but the old man found unexpected strength in his body. He crushed her to him, forced his hot face down to hers.

Laura screamed and struck him with her fist. His mouth touched her face and she shrank in aversion from his lips. Fugger released one of his hands to grab her face and force it up to his and that gave Laura her opportunity.

She wrenched away from him and slapped his face. Fugger staggered back, a look of incredible rage on his face.

"Why, damn you!" he mouthed.

He took a sudden step forward, raised his hand and clenching it into a fist, smashed her in the face.

Laura was knocked to her knees and remained on them for a moment. Then she picked herself up. Fugger stared at her.

"I'll be going now," Laura said, coldly.

She opened the door.

"Wait!" cried Fugger, in panic. "Wait—I'll apologize—I'll—"

Laura went out and started down the stairs. Fugger hurried after her. "I'll double your salary!" he called after her.

Laura continued down the stairs, walked through the store and went out of the front door. Fugger stood on the stairs looking after her. When the door slammed he began swearing low and furiously.

Chapter 22

The stage coach swirled up before the Turkey Crossing station in a cloud of dust and the middle-aged station attendant promptly began unhitching the horses.

Laura Vesser climbed down from the stage. She stood for a moment, her eyes looking off beyond the stage station.

Tancred came up, leading the fresh horses. He saw Laura, but did not speak to her. For a moment or two Tancred and the agent were busy, unhitching and hitching up the fresh team. The stage driver went around to the boot and took out a valise. He brought it to Laura and dropped it at her feet.

"Here you are, Miss!"

He climbed back on his perch, waited until Tancred hitched up the last trace. Then he shouted, "Hiyah!"

The horses sprang forward and the coach started off. Then the agent turned to Laura, his face perplexed. "You're staying here, ma'am?" Then, as she nodded, "There ain't no 'commodations here for people."

"I know," she said, "but my name is Laura Vesser and I'd hoped you could put me up until the next stage."

The agent gave a start and his eyes darted in the direction of the grave behind the station. He said in a sympathetic tone, "I think we might manage, ma'am."

Leaving her bag on the ground, Laura walked around the stage station, back to her father's grave. When she returned, the stage was several miles away and Tancred had already rubbed down and fed the tired horses. He was coming out of the corral and met Laura a short distance from the station.

He said, "Did you know I was here?"

"How could I know? You left Sage City without telling —anyone—where you were going."

"You've left—for good?"

129

"I'm going back east. I just stopped off here to . . ." Her eyes went to the mound behind the stage station.

Her eyes returned to his after a moment and she smiled faintly. "I want to wash up." She started away, then stopped. "You know that Luke Miller was killed right after you left?"

He could not conceal a start and she went on into the stage station. For long moments, Tancred remained standing where she had left him, then he finally turned and went into the barn. He sat on the edge of the horse manger, one leg swinging loosely and kicking the boards with its heel.

He sat there for a long time, until Waxman, the agent, came out and called to him, "Grub's ready."

He followed the other man to the station. The table was set and Laura was helping the agent's wife bring the food in from the kitchen. It was a better meal than usual, with hot biscuits, but it was eaten in complete silence by all four.

When he had finished eating, Tancred went out and took care of the horses. He worked for an hour or more, then came out of the corral and found Laura standing nearby.

"Who killed him?" he asked.

"No one knows who fired the gun. Fugger and Smith say it was . . . you."

"That's nonsense! Miller meant more to me than any man I've met in . . . in years."

"They say you killed him because he found out who you were."

"They know . . . everyone?"

"Yes."

He was silent for a moment, but a little frown grew on his face, a frown that had seldom come on his features, usually cold and impassive. "What do you think?"

"I don't think—I *know*—that you didn't kill him."

"What's Mrs. Miller doing?"

"What can she do?"

Tancred hesitated. "I thought perhaps she'd keep on with the paper."

"That's a man's job."

"Women have run newspapers."

"Not in Sage City, not with Jacob Fugger owning the

town." It was her turn to hesitate. "I—I had a quarrel with him." She bit her lower lip. "He struck me."

"Why?" cried Tancred.

She shook her head in confusion, was silent. Hard knots of muscle stood out on his jaws.

"I misjudged him. He *was* interested in something else than money and power." He drew a slow breath. "Who's mayor of Sage?"

"Who else?"

"How could he be? His term was up. Even with Miller dead. What about the city council?"

"What council?"

"So it's like that. But ... Lee Kinnaird?"

"He arrested Hong Kong Smith and a mob broke into the jail and turned him loose."

"Lee?" exclaimed Tancred.

"He was hurt, but he's all right. He—he says you left Sage City because you were afraid that your staying would hurt Mr. Miller—when people knew you were Wes Tancred. . . ." She paused. "Good night—Wes."

She turned and walked toward the stage station. Tancred went back to the corral and leaning over the top poles stared sightlessly at the horses inside.

Later, when the light went out inside the station he walked back to Vesser's grave. He stood there in the darkness for long minutes and after a while his lips moved slightly.

Words came from his mouth, "There's no end to it!"

After a while he turned away. He walked toward the corral with certain steps and swinging open the gate went inside and found his own horse.

He led it out and saddled it in front of the stable. He looped his carpetbag over the horn and swung up into the saddle.

He rode past the stage station at a careful walk and did not see Laura Vesser standing in the dark open doorway. Laura watched him ride away, then went into the station.

Chapter 23

It was shortly after seven o'clock on Thursday morning when Tancred rode down South Street in Sage City. There were only a few people on the street at this early hour, but one or two stopped and stared at him, as he rode by, looking neither to the right or the left.

The waitress at the Bon Ton Café saw him through the window and came running out of the restaurant to look after him. Horace Van Meter, who was having trouble with his accounts at the bank and had gotten up early to work on them, stopped a dozen feet from his destination and whistled softly as he saw Tancred.

Tancred rode to the cross street and turned to the right. He stopped in front of the *Star* plant and looked inside. It was deserted.

He stepped away from the door and looked toward the Miller home. Then, drawing a deep breath, he started walking toward it.

He knocked on the door and it was opened by Mrs. Miller. For a moment she stared at him in astonishment, then a low cry was torn from her throat and she leaned against him. Tancred put his arm about her shoulder and she put her head on his chest and sobbed.

"I didn't do it, Mrs. Miller," Tancred said, quietly.

She raised her tear-stained face. "I know you didn't. It was . . . Jacob Fugger. I—I always felt that it would come to that, but Luke wouldn't listen. He was that way. He was afraid . . . I knew he was always afraid, but he wouldn't stop. . . ." She stopped and dabbed at her eyes with the skirt of her apron. Then she cleared her throat.

"Come in, John. I'll make some breakfast. . . ."

He followed her into the house. It was spotlessly clean, although the furniture was sparse and of poor quality; some of it seemed to have been made by Miller himself.

"Sit down," Mrs. Miller said, pointing to a rocking chair. "That was Luke's. . . ."

She winced, then to recover, bustled about the stove. "Coffee's ready and I'll have some eggs and ham in a jiffy. There's some fresh bread that I made last night."

She looked at him. "I didn't have much time to make home-made bread before, there was always so much work, but now . . . now, I've got nothing but time."

"What are you going to do . . . about the paper?"

"We owed some money on the equipment; they'll take it. The rest. . . . Mose thought perhaps I could sell it to the newspaper at Dodge or Ellsworth."

"No," said Tancred. "Keep the newspaper."

"But I can't run it—alone."

"I'll help you."

She stared at him. For a moment a ray of hope showed in her eyes but then it faded and she shook her head. "It wouldn't work. It would only be the same thing over again."

"Perhaps, but Fugger'll know it, this time," Tancred said.

A little shudder ran through Mrs. Miller. "But that's just revenge. And—and then you'll be like Luke—dead—and no one will be any the better for it."

"The town will," said Tancred. "And perhaps some of the people. People who've been frightened by Fugger, intimidated. I think," he added, slowly, "that was the way Mr. Miller thought about. He—he knew that he was risking his life and still—he kept on."

"I know." Mrs. Miller looked thoughtfully at Tancred. "We can get out a paper today," he said.

"We missed last week," she mused aloud, "and there's a lot of the local stuff still standing. We could do without the ads, or perhaps just run some of the old ones to fill up space. . . ." She turned suddenly and went to a shelf beside the stove. She took down a large key and extended it to Tancred.

"Here's the key. After breakfast I'll find Mose and I'll come down to the shop myself."

Tancred unlocked the door of the *Star* shop and went inside. He set his carpetbag down beside Miller's desk, got some paper and a pencil. Words had been pouring through his mind and he began to write.

He wrote a heading, in large letters, *"Jacob Fugger Murdered Luke Miller."* Then below he began to write:

"Jacob Fugger, last week, murdered Luke Miller, the publisher of this newspaper. Fugger didn't fire the gun that killed Miller, but he pointed the hand that pulled the trigger and he paid for the bullet that killed Miller.

"Jacob Fugger has robbed and cheated the people of this community long enough. For his own selfish reasons he has aided and abetted trouble-makers and killers. The men who gallop the streets of Sage City, who fire their guns and injure and kill people are here because of Jacob Fugger. Fugger encourages and protects them and when a man dares to speak out against Fugger, he is shot down in cold blood. . . ."

He was still writing when Mose Hudkins came in and quietly went to the rear of the long room and began to work. A few minutes later, Mrs. Miller entered. Tancred got up and handed her the article he had written.

Mrs. Miller read it carefully. When she had completed reading, she nodded. "We'll use the biggest type we can."

An hour later Lee Kinnaird came into the print shop. "Can I talk to you, Wes?" he asked.

Tancred shook his head. "Later. We've got to get out a newspaper today." Then he grimaced. "Is it important, Lee?"

Kinnaird hesitated. "It'll wait."

He went out.

The were no other callers that day, although once when Tancred was in front he looked through the window and saw Gil Packard walking past on the far side of the street. Packard was looking toward the newspaper shop.

The boy brought the bundle of newspapers into Fugger's store and Fugger, who was standing just inside the door, grabbed them from him. He peeled off one paper and let the others drop to the floor. His eyes took in the headline and a groan escaped his lips. He read on, his face slowly turning pale.

At the back of his store, Gil Packard finished reading

the front page of the *Star*. He stood for a moment,
staring at the newspaper, then got his hat and went out.
He did not bother to lock the door behind him. There had
been no customers in the store for two days and it was
unlikely that any would come now.

Herb Glassman was standing up in his tiny little
office, across from the courthouse, reading the paper when
the door opened and Gil Packard came in. Packard pointed
to the paper.

"What do you think?"

"He's committing suicide, that's what I think," said
Herb.

"It took a lot to even come back to Sage City."

Glassman frowned. "Let's go over and see Judge Kraft."

They left the little office, crossed the street and
climbed the stairs to the courtroom on the second floor.
Judge Kraft was the only person in the big room and
there was an open newspaper on the table before which
he sat, although he was not reading it at the moment.

Mose Hudkins had cleaned up and left the shop. Mrs.
Miller was washing her hands at the rear. She dried them
on a towel. "Come to the house for supper," she said.

"Not tonight," replied Tancred. He indicated the cot.
"I'll sleep here, but before I go to bed I've got to show
myself around town."

"Is that wise?" Mrs. Miller asked, worriedly.

"I think it's necessary."

She hesitated, but she had committed herself and she
had to go through with it. She said, "Good night, Wes."

"Good night, Mrs. Miller."

She went out.

Tancred picked up his carpetbag, which still stood beside the late publisher's desk and carried it to the cot at
the rear of the shop. He set it down and opened it up
and then he heard the door open. He whirled, then
relaxed.

A group of men were coming into the shop. Gil
Packard was in the lead. Tancred recognized the others
as Judge Kraft, Prosecutor Glassman and two men who
had been elected to the city council along with the others.

"Mr. Tancred," said Gil Packard, as the spokesman

for the group, "we're here because we've all just read this week's *Star*."

Tancred regarded Packard narrowly. "Yes?"

"We represent the duly elected officials of Sage City and the County of Sage. We were legally elected and although we haven't as yet performed any duties we intend to do so. . . ." He paused to moisten his lips. "That is, on one condition."

Tancred waited. Packard shot a quick look around his little group, saw that no one had weakened and drew a deep breath. "On condition that you accept the job of town marshal. . . ."

Tancred stared at them. "You know that I am Wes Tancred?"

"We know it."

The door opened again and Lee Kinnaird came in. Tancred said, "Lee, they want me to be marshal."

"Have they promised you any special kind of funeral?" Kinnaird held aloft a copy of the *Star*. "I've just read this."

"If necessary, we'll form a Vigilante committee," Packard said, angrily.

"Then you don't need a marshal," Tancred said quickly.

Herb Glassman stepped forward. He threw up his hand. "Wait a minute, Tancred. There'll be no Vigilante committee. I'll go along with the rest on most anything—as long as it's legal. But just because Jacob Fugger's broken every law in the book doesn't mean that we should. . . ."

Judge Kraft cleared his throat. "Glassman's right, we've got to uphold the law."

Kinnaird touched the bandage on his head. "Last week I arrested a man named Smith. I did it quite legal-like and he was taken away from me in a very *un*legal-like manner." He pointed to Glassman. "Did you issue any warrants, Prosecutor?" He whirled on Judge Kraft. "Did you sentence anyone last week, Judge?" He turned back to Tancred. "Don't do it, Wes. They'll let you go out and face Eric Stratemeyer and Dave Helm and they'll be behind you . . . a long ways behind. So far behind that the bullets can't hit them."

Packard asked savagely, "Have you gone over to Fugger's side, Kinnaird?"

Kinnaird grinned crookedly and walked out of the

shop. When the door was closed the councilmen looked uneasily at one another. Tancred drew a deep breath.

"I've thrown it in Fugger's teeth. I've got to back it up . . . I'll take the job. . . ."

The councilmen shouted and began to converge on Tancred. He held up his hand. "I'll take the badge, but I'm warning you—I won't give it back until it's all over. I mean that, no matter how quickly you change your minds, I'll see it through."

"*I* won't quit!" shouted Gil Packard. "I promise you that."

Tancred walked back to the cot and reaching in, took out a heavy bundle. He unrolled it, exposing his Navy Colt. "This gun," he told his visitors, "is the gun that killed Sam Older. I'm telling you that now because it's going to be thrown into your faces . . . that I'm the man who killed Sam Older. Yes, I killed him. I'll tell you this, too. There was no deal. I received no reward for killing Older. I killed him to keep him from killing me. There are no charges against me—anywhere. That's as much as I'm going to say about myself—and Sam Older. I thought you ought to hear it from me."

He spun the cylinder of the revolver, saw that it was working smoothly and thrust the gun under the waistband of his trousers. Nodding to the councilmen he went past them and left the shop.

On South Street, Tancred crossed to the jail. As he neared the door it was opened and Chuck Gorey stepped out.

"Well, if it ain't Mr. Tancred," Gorey said, thinly.

"Give me your badge, Gorey," Tancred said. "You're through as marshal of Sage City."

"What?" gasped Gorey then his face turned a sudden crimson. "What're you trying to pull?"

"The city council's appointed me marshal," Tancred said in a deadly calm voice.

"What city council? I mean—they got no right."

Tancred held out his hand. "Give me your badge."

Gorey's eyes dropped to the revolver, the first time he had ever seen Tancred with a gun. A sudden whine came into his voice. "You're trying to make me draw on you . . ."

"For the last time, give me that badge!"

A palsy shook Gorey and he had trouble unpinning the badge. He handed it to Tancred, his hand shaking. Tancred took it and pinned it on his shirt. "Put your keys on the desk inside," he said evenly. "Then get out—and don't cross me, because if you do, I'll kill you."

He turned and walked away. Gorey stared at his back and the temptation to draw his gun and shoot Tancred must have been terrible. But something kept him from doing it; fear that Tancred, in spite of a bullet in his back, would still kill him.

Tancred walked perhaps thirty yards, then crossed the street. He passed McCoy's Saloon, the hotel and the Texas Saloon. Finally he came to Fugger's store. Without breaking his stride he turned in and opened the door.

There were two or three customers in the store, but Fugger was nowhere in sight. Tancred walked through the store and a sudden hush fell in the big room. He climbed the stairs to the balcony and pushed open the door of Fugger's private office.

Fugger sat at his desk, some account books in front of him. He gave a violent start as he recognized Tancred.

"You!"

"You're under arrest, Fugger," Tancred said evenly.

Sheer horror spread over Fugger's face. "What— what are you talking about?"

"I'm arresting you for the murder of Luke Miller," Tancred said. "You're coming to jail with me."

"You're crazy!" Fugger cried hoarsely. "You can't—"

"I'd rather kill you," Tancred went on, "but Luke Miller wanted things done according to the law, so come with me."

Fugger pushed back his chair and got to his feet. "Where?" he gasped.

"Jail."

"You'd put *me* in jail?"

Tancred stood aside and gestured to the door. Fugger swayed for a moment, then reeled toward the door. He went down the stairs, almost stumbling a couple of times.

Downstairs the customers and his clerks watched in awe as Fugger, followed closely by Tancred, walked through the store, to the door.

On the street, people came out of stores, watched as Fugger shuffled along. As they neared McCoy's Saloon, Fugger's steps faltered. Tancred reached out and gave him a shove. Fugger almost fell on his face. He cried out, recovered and almost ran ahead of Tancred.

Hong Kong Smith, half-sober, stared at Tancred as he passed. Then he turned to a cowboy. "Get Dave Helm and Manny Harpending." He saw McCoy's face over the batwing doors. "Get Eric Stratemeyer."

Fugger marched into the marshal's office and stopped. Tancred indicated the door leading to the cell in the rear.

"Not in there," sobbed Fugger.

Tancred opened the door and shoved Fugger in violently. Then he turned the key in the door.

As he came out of the marshal's office, Lee Kinnaird came up. "So you've done it!"

Tancred nodded. "I'll be back in a little while . . . to face them."

He walked down the street, cutting diagonally across, so that he reached the far sidewalk in front of McCoy's Saloon. Hong Kong Smith stood outside the door. His face was coldly savage.

"You've got an hour to get out of town," said Tancred.

"You've got about a half hour—to live!" retorted Hong Kong Smith.

Tancred went on to the Texas Saloon. He entered.

Lily Leeds was behind the bar, but when she saw Tancred her face paled and she walked to her office. Tancred followed her into the little room and closed the door.

"She found you!" Lily said.

"Laura? Yes."

"You love her, Wes! Then why didn't you go away with her? Why did you come back?"

"What else could I do, Lily? I couldn't run—any more. A man's got to make a stand somewhere."

"You can't fight them all. There are too many."

"I've got Fugger and he gives the orders. He'll be the first to die . . . and I think he's afraid to die." He looked at her sharply. "I just wanted to ask you one question . . . what's happened to Lee Kinnaird?"

"What do you mean, Wes?"

"He's . . . different."

"Oh, he had a rather hard time of it while you were gone. He arrested Hong Kong Smith."

"I know about that. That wouldn't change him."

"Well, maybe he thinks the situation is hopeless . . ." Then, as Tancred started to turn away, "Wait . . . !"

He stopped and looked at her.

She said, "He's in love with Laura Vesser. He . . . he hates you."

He let out a heavy sigh and opened the door. Lily cried out, "Wes . . . !"

He went out.

Chapter 24

When he came out of the saloon, Tancred saw a knot of
Texas men gathered around Hong Kong Smith. It was a
quiet group, however. They watched him as he crossed
the street, but no one spoke, no one made a move.

He went on to the courthouse. Kinnaird stepped out as
he came up. Behind Tancred, down the street, horses came
galloping.

Kinnaird said, "Fugger offered me ten thousand dollars to turn him loose."

"He made me an offer once," Tancred said. "He said
every man had a price."

Kinnaird, looking past Tancred, nodded. "They're coming."

Tancred stepped aside, made a half turn, to that he
was facing Kinnaird and could look down the street. The
horsemen had come to a halt in front of McCoy's Saloon
and were dismounting. Hong Kong Smith and his other
group had merged with them. The augmented force began
to move on foot, diagonally across the street, toward the
jail.

Hong Kong Smith walked in front. At his left were
Manny Harpending and Dave Helm. On his right was
Eric Stratemeyer, coatless, the cheap, nickel-plated revolver conspicuous in its holster. Behind the quartet came
the Texas men.

Chuck Gorey came around the side of the jail, saw
Tancred and stopped.

Tancred said, "I thought you might miss it, Gorey."

Sudden fear showed on Gorey's face. He started to back
away, but Tancred halted him. "Stand still." He nodded
to Kinnaird.

"Bring out Fugger."

Kinnaird waited a brief moment. "I can't. I let him
out the back way."

"So ten thousand *was* your price!"

"No," said Kinnaird. "It wasn't the money. It was . . ."

"Never mind. It's too late."

He took another backward step and Kinnaird moved out of the doorway, across from Tancred.

A dozen feet away Hong Kong Smith stopped.

"Your half hour's up," he growled.

Gil Packard, Prosecutor Glassman, Judge Kraft and the other men who had called on Tancred a half hour ago, came around the corner and started across the street.

"Hold everything!" Packard called out.

Without looking at them, Tancred said, sharply, "Keep out of this. It's my fight."

Eric Stratemeyer pointed. "Is that the gun with which you killed Sam Older?" His voice was a taunt, the challenge from which there was no turning back.

"In spite of his faults," Tancred said, taking it up, "Sam Older never asked for the odds."

Stung, Stratemeyer sneered. "Look who's talking . . . the yellow-bellied coward who shot Sam Older in the back. . . ." He pursed up his lips and began to whistle the tune of the ballad of Sam Older.

Dave Helm said, suddenly, thickly, "Hong Kong, I didn't bargain for this." He took a quick step forward, made a half turn to face the Texas men. "I'll kill the first man who makes a move. . . ."

Still whistling, Stratemeyer's hand streaked for his gun.

He was fast, terribly fast, yet nine years ago, Tancred would have beaten him. But the years told and Stratemeyer's gun was in his hand, spouting flame and lead, when Tancred's came up.

It was the speed of the draw and the fast triggering that was so necessary to a professional gunfighter of Stratemeyer's calibre that beat him. He drew fast and he fired fast, but his aim was not true enough. He counted entirely on his speed. His first bullet missed Tancred by a hair's breadth and his second tore through Tancred's shirt and barely grazed his skin. There was no third bullet, for Tancred's caught him squarely between the eyes.

Tancred made his half-swivel, caught Kinnaird with his gun just clearing the holster. Kinnaird, in that last instant of his life, saw his fate and started to cry out. Tancred's bullet choked it off.

Harpending went for his gun only a fraction of an instant

after Stratemeyer, but he never quite got his gun out. Dave Helm's bullet caught him in the stomach and Harpending, gasping, folded forward.

Hong Kong Smith, the big, booming man from Texas, was suddenly paralyzed. His hands went halfway up and he babbled: "Don't shoot—don't shoot—"

His lips twisted into a sneer, Dave Helm stepped forward. He thrust out his gun so that the muzzle was almost touching Smith. He said, "This is the way I gave it to Luke Miller . . ." and pulled the trigger.

Tancred turned on Chuck Gorey. The ex-marshal stood, his mouth wide open in fright, his hand frozen, the fingers crooked, halfway to his gun.

"Go ahead, Gorey!" snapped Tancred. "Make your play!"

But Gorey could not move.

Then Jacob Fugger, the middle-aged book-keeper turned tycoon, hurtled out from between the jail and the adjoining building. There was a gun in his hand, and saliva drooling from his mouth. His eyes, the eyes of a madman, were straight ahead.

And straight ahead of him, his back turned to Fugger, was Dave Helm.

Fugger pulled the trigger. Tancred saw the bullet hit Helm, hurl him forward to his knees. He turned his gun on Fugger, but held his fire.

Slowly, with great effort and agony on his face, Dave Helm twisted around. His gun came up—thundered. Fugger let out an unearthly scream and hit the earth. His legs thrashed wildly.

Helm's tortured face came up. His eyes met Tancred's across the distance.

"Good-bye, Wes!" he choked.

"Good-bye, Dave," said Tancred, soberly. He started forward but Helm's eyes glazed and he fell forward on his face.

Not one of the Texas men drew a gun. Dave Helm's defection had stopped them. Or, perhaps, they were men, like Helm, who didn't like the odds—if they were against the other man.

Tancred stepped out and turned. He cocked his head to one side and watched Gil Packard come slowly forward. Shock showed on the merchant's face.

"It's over," said Tancred. He looked at Packard, then

at the Texas men who still stood where they had stopped behind Hong Kong Smith.

He raised the gun that had killed Sam Older and realized that he no longer had any aversion for it. He felt very tired, but an odd peace had come over him.

Then his eyes went beyond the Texas men, up the street. Far away, past Fugger's Store, he saw a swiftly running figure, a girl. Behind her, at the depot, was the morning train from the east.

A half smile came over Tancred's face. He thrust the revolver under his waistband and took off the marshal's badge that he had pinned on less than a half hour ago.

"I won't need this any more," he said. He tossed it to Gil Packard. Packard tried to catch it, but missed and stooped to pick it up from the ground. When he straightened with the badge in his hand, Tancred had gone away.

He was walking down the street, toward Laura Vesser, who was coming from the train toward him.

They met ten feet from the door of the Texas Saloon. Lily Leeds standing in the doorway, looked at them for a moment, then turned and went back into the saloon.